Love Directions

A GOOD BAD IDEA NOVEL

ARIELLA ZOELLE

Copyright © 2020 A.F. Zoelle/Ariella Zoelle

Published by Sarayashi Publishing

www.ariellazoelle.com

All rights reserved.

This is a work of fiction. Names, characters, places, and incidents are products of the author's imagination or used fictitiously. Any resemblance to actual persons, living or dead, is purely coincidental. All products and brand names are registered trademarks of their respective holders/companies.

This book or any portion thereof may not be reproduced or used in any manner whatsoever without the express written permission of the publisher except for the use of brief quotations in a book review.

Cover Design by Cate of Cate Ashwood Designs

Editing by Pam of Undivided Editing

Proofreading by Sandra of One Love Editing

Layout by Ariella of Sarayashi Publishing

ISBN: 978-1-954202-00-9

Dedication

For those who have lost loved ones to cancer.

Author's Note

The **Good Bad Idea** series can be read in any order. However, North is first mentioned in Chapter 9 of **Love Means More**, and appears in Chapter 8 of **Fancy Love**. If you would like to see where Elias's story began, please refer to **Love Fool**. This book starts a little over three months after its epilogue.

Welcome to Sunnyside!

Immerse yourself in the world of interconnected series set in the fictional town of Sunnyside

Full of cute sweetness and sexy fun, every story ends with a satisfying HEA and no cliffhangers. Since all of the following series are set in the same town, you can expect to see cameos of your favorite characters! The books are funny, steamy, and can be read in any order.

To access the Sunnyside universe reading order guide, please visit www.ariellazoelle.com/sunnyside

Chapter One

ELIAS

AS SOON AS I sat at the bar, Red came over to greet me. Short, spunky, and with fiery auburn hair, it was easy to see how he earned the nickname. "Hey, Elias! How's it going?"

"Pretty good, actually. How are you?"

"Happy to see you, as always." He flashed a charming smile at me that made me wonder not for the first time why I couldn't have fallen for him instead of my cheating ex, Josh. "Do you want your usual?"

"That would be wonderful, thanks." As I watched him make my peach sour, I relaxed as the stress from work left me. "How's Gonk doing?"

Gonk was the nickname of Red's cat, Algonquin, who was named after the famous New York City hotel's cat and their whiskey martini. "He's doing great! I'm struggling to teach him to jump up on command, which is going about as well as you would expect."

"Which means terribly?"

Red laughed as he set my drink in front of me. "That's the nice way of putting it. Unmitigated disaster is probably closer to the truth. The only trick he's mastered so far is making me give him treats to not do tricks."

"You always said he was a smart cat."

"We'll see who out-stubborns who in the end." Red chuckled to himself as he wiped down the bar counter. "My money's on Gonk, personally. I'm too much of a pushover with him."

"When he's that cute, it's hard not to be."

"I know, right? I have the same problem with men." Red tucked his towel into his black apron tied around his waist. "So, what does my horoscope predict is in my future?"

After Mom passed away, I missed her giving me the daily update on what her horoscope predicted for us. At first, I had checked them as a way of feeling close to her again. Now, it was a comforting habit that I found mildly embarrassing.

Red had discovered it when he saw me checking on my phone once. Whether he was being polite or was genuinely interested was unclear, but I never felt like he was making fun of me when he asked about his horoscope.

I pulled up the Signs of the Times website to read

his. "Today is the day you can change someone's life, Taurus. In helping others, you will help yourself. Don't be afraid to give a friend the push they need to overcome their obstacles. They will thank you in the long run. Playing Cupid will bring happiness into everyone's lives."

"Playing Cupid? Sounds like fun."

I savored my drink, which was sweet despite "sour" being in the name. "Just be careful about where you land your arrow. Some of us have had enough terrible partners to last us for the rest of our lives."

"Ugh, tell me about it. My last boyfriend was more interested in his fantasy football team than being with me." Red groaned at the memory. "Ranking seventeenth in importance behind sixteen virtual men on a spreadsheet really bruises your ego. But enough about Darren. What's your horoscope say?"

"You're going to meet a stranger today who will change your life, Virgo. Don't be apprehensive about opening yourself up to romantic possibilities. It could bring you a lifetime of love and happiness if you let it." Yeah, right. Like that would happen to someone as unlucky as me.

"If I didn't know any better, it sure sounds like I'm supposed to play Cupid and bring a stranger into your life to be your new boyfriend."

I laughed at the ridiculous notion. "There's no

chance of that happening. Callum is meeting me here soon, and he's already dating someone amazing." His boyfriend was Rune Tourneau, a famous model who was so beautiful that it was almost impossible to believe he really existed. Even if I had been interested in Callum that way, I never would have stood a chance against an Adonis like Rune.

"Yeah, but he's not a stranger. This is someone new and exciting who might change your life."

When the front door opened, I glanced over to check if it was Callum arriving. A guy in his early twenties entered and headed over our way. Dressed in jeans and a blue T-shirt, he looked like the cute boy next door that all moms wished you would bring home. He had wavy blond hair that made you crave to run your fingers through it, which framed his angular face. He took a seat on the end of the bar. "Red, you're just the man I wanted to see tonight!"

"You say that every night you come here."

"That's because it's always true." His broad grin was the kind that caused you to smile along with him. It gave him a roguish charm, which was a great look on him. "What magical cocktail do you have for me to try tonight?"

"One that will probably have you making cockpit jokes." Red set about preparing a drink for him.

"You know I love a good cock joke."

"I'm pretty sure you love a good cock, with or without the joke."

He laughed heartily at Red's quip, although my cheeks flushed. I wasn't a prude, but I was easily embarrassed. A lot of my discomfort stemmed from my terrible experiences. My two boyfriends had both been older than me, which I had assumed would make them more mature and stable. Instead, they had both been callous and moody, constantly expecting sex, whether or not I enjoyed it. Will had been mediocre at best, but Josh's rough aggression had been uncomfortable to endure. I could only assume that my lack of pleasure from being with them was because something was wrong with me. It was why I was gun-shy about pursuing another relationship; I wasn't in any rush to get hurt again.

The man's cheeky expression was adorable. "Guilty as charged."

I stiffened when Red's attention shifted to me. He tilted his head at the other customer. "Maybe he could be your stranger?"

"I'm hardly a stranger." The man scoffed at the notion. "I've been coming here for ages."

"True, but you're a stranger to Elias." Red used a shaker to mix the ingredients, before pouring out a beautiful lavender drink into a chilled martini glass. He garnished it with a flamed lemon peel before setting it down by the empty chair beside me. "Why don't you come over here to enjoy your aviation cocktail while you get to know him?"

"Sure. What's in it?" When the man's gaze met

mine, I felt an unexpected electric jolt spark inside me. He got up and walked over to take a seat next to me. It amazed me he was even more attractive up close, with stunning blue-green eyes that flustered me when he glanced at me with a sexy half-smile.

"Gin, maraschino liqueur, crème de violette, and lemon juice."

He took a sip, his eyebrows arching up in surprise at the flavor. "It almost tastes floral, but I like it! The maraschino and lemon balance it out nicely. And you're right, the aviation and cockpit jokes write themselves."

"Elias, this is North. He's another regular of mine."

North shook my hand as he introduced himself, sending currents zinging through me as we touched. "I'm North Easton. Nice to meet you, Elias."

That was quite an interesting name. "North *East*on?"

"Yeah, and my twin is West Easton. There isn't a joke about that we haven't heard." He grinned, even though he was probably sick of everyone having the same response. "If you think that's bad, my mom has a cat called Woof. My theory is she's overcompensating for being named Linda."

He said it with a straight face, but I couldn't believe him. "You're joking, right?"

"I wish I was. When she was a kid, she had a Chihuahua named Meow."

It was so absurd I had to laugh. "Now you're just messing with me."

North pulled out his phone and opened his group text with his mother and sister. He scrolled up a bit to a picture of a very regal-looking gray Siamese cat wearing a gold crown and white fur-lined purple velvet cloak. The texts under it made me snicker.

> MOM
>
> King Woof requests your presence at dinner.
>
> WEST
>
> Kings don't make requests; they command.
>
> MOM
>
> Fine, he commands you to stop being a smart-ass.
>
> Good luck with that. Does Lord Woofie have a specific time in mind?

The conversation was so delightfully weird. "I bet her next cat's name is Mouse."

"You're probably right. That's absolutely her sense of humor."

I raised my drink in a toast. "Congratulations, you're officially the most interesting person I know now."

"I'm honored." He clinked his glass against mine. "So, what's this I hear about me being your stranger?"

As he drank his cocktail while watching me, I

found myself tongue-tied. Thankfully, Red answered for me. "His horoscope said he would meet a stranger that would change his life today. It also suggested that he should be open to the possibility of love, hint hint. Mine said I should play Cupid, so this seems like the perfect trifecta to make magic happen."

It was embarrassing having my horoscope habit being revealed. I hurried to justify my interest. "Horoscopes were my mom's thing."

North studied me, his gaze piercing through me as if he could see all my secrets somehow. I felt exposed but remained silent as I waited for him to respond. He took another sip before he shocked me. "You must be a Virgo."

I blinked at him in disbelief. "How could you tell?"

His cryptic smile did funny things to my heart. "I'm magic."

"If you're so magical, what am I?" Red challenged.

"Oh, you're definitely a Taurus. There's no question about that."

His accuracy was uncanny, further intriguing me. "Why do you know that?"

"I told you: I'm magic." He stated it with so much confidence, I almost believed him. Who was this guy?

Red didn't seem nearly as impressed as I was. "Why do I suspect it has more to do with West being into that stuff?"

"Hey, I thought you were supposed to be playing Cupid. You're ruining my attempt at being a mysterious stranger."

Red snorted as he leaned his hip against the bar. "Is that what you're trying to do? Could have fooled me."

"Fine, if you must know, several people in my family read horoscopes on Signs of the Times because my aunt works there."

"Does she write the horoscopes?" My mental image of the writer was an older woman with long gray hair, surrounded by a lot of healing crystals, who smelled of patchouli incense and wore bohemian clothes.

"No, she's the IT manager in charge of their website maintenance."

It was a disappointing answer. It would have been neat to hear how they wrote horoscopes. "She does an outstanding job. Most of the other astrology sites look like they were built in the late 1990s and haven't been updated since. Signs of the Times actually looks as if it was made this decade."

"Trust me, she had to drag them kicking and screaming into the redesign. For folks who deal with predicting the future, you'd think they'd be more interested in living in it."

"I guess some people are just too set in their old ways."

The door opened as Callum entered the restaurant, bringing the sunshine with him in his smile. He was adorable as usual with a pink gingham bow tie paired with a lavender shirt and jeans. With his baby face and lilting Irish brogue, he was a total sweetheart. I was lucky to call him my friend.

North stunned me by greeting him before I could. "Hey, Callum! What're you doing here?"

Callum hugged him before saying hi to me. "I'm having dinner with Elias tonight. I didn't realize you were friends with him, too."

"We just met. Red is attempting to play Cupid for us."

Callum's dark blue eyes went wide with surprise. "Oh!"

"How do you two know each other?" I asked.

"My brother's boyfriend, Augie, has a younger brother named Felix. When I first moved here, Felix introduced me to his friends, and North was one of them because they're roommates. We've been friends ever since."

Sometimes it surprised me what a small world it was. "That's great."

"North, do you want to join us? I mean, if that's okay with you, Elias."

"Thanks, but I shouldn't crash your dinner plans." His refusal was unexpectedly disappointing.

Maybe it was the horoscope influencing me, or maybe it was the fact that North was handsome and intriguing, but I wished I could talk to him more. For someone as introverted as me, it was hard to put myself out there, but something in my gut told me it would be worth it. I nervously adjusted my glasses as I took an uncharacteristic risk. "I'd enjoy talking with you further, if you'd like to join us."

When North hesitated, Callum chided him. "Since when are you the shy one?"

"I'm not being shy. I'm trying to be polite."

Red scoffed. "Why start now?"

North shot him a look before he returned his attention to us. "Sure, if you feel like putting up with me, I'm in."

Callum brightened at his friend agreeing to have dinner with us. "In that case, we should probably get a table."

"Go grab one, and I'll send your server over," Red offered. "Enjoy your meal!"

As North and I collected our drinks to move, I held Red's gaze. "Thank you."

He winked at me. "Thank me after you fall in love with him."

I blushed at that but said nothing as I walked toward the booth. Sitting next to Callum with North across from us, I couldn't wait to see what else the evening had in store for me.

Chapter Two

NORTH

I WAS an instalust kind of guy. The Japanese word *"menkui"* described me perfectly: someone who was attracted to the way somebody looked. When I saw a gorgeous man, sex was always the first thing on my mind. My priority was having fun and getting laid as often as possible, which meant hooking up with frat boys who were down to hit it and quit it. Romance wasn't conducive to getting my rocks off, so I never worried about it. It was great my buddy Callum had found true love with his boyfriend, Rune, but that shit wasn't for me.

Or at least it wasn't until I saw Elias. He was so beautiful I couldn't look away from him. With normal hot guys, I'd steal covert looks at them while fantasizing about them sucking my dick in the men's room. But Elias was a work of art that I marveled could exist in this fucked-up world. His white-blond hair gave him an angelic appearance, and he was rocking the chic-nerd look with his well-tailored suit and rimless glasses. His gray eyes were so pretty that if I were a musician, I would've written a song about them.

Between his horoscope predicting my arrival and being friends with Callum, it seemed like an epic sign from the cosmic universe that we should be with each other. As cute as he was, I was more than ready to accept such a generous gift from destiny. Was that what instalove felt like? Was that why I wanted to not only fuck him, but cuddle with him afterward?

But I had never done anything other than casual hookups before. I didn't have a clue about how I was supposed to make whatever this was happen. Sitting across from him at the table with Callum, I was having a hard enough time not losing my shit over how precious he was. Keeping my cool was a serious challenge when I was desperate to give a good first impression. I doubted making googly eyes at him was the best way to do that.

Wanting to find out more about Elias, I asked, "How did you two become friends?"

"Elias is an attorney at our company, so we've gotten to know each other pretty well over the past couple of months."

"Wow, so that means you're supersmart, then."

I never knew that someone pushing glasses up the bridge of their nose could be so sexy until he did it.

"Only about book things. I wish I could say the same thing about real life."

His modesty was endearing. "You're probably not giving yourself enough credit."

"He's definitely not," Callum agreed.

A slight blush graced Elias's cheeks, which was cute as hell. I had always been attracted to outgoing, boisterous bros who liked to bang, so being interested in such a shy guy was an unfamiliar experience for me. It was clear he wished to get away from being the topic of conversation. "What do you do?"

"I'm a university student, double majoring in art and creative writing."

"He's incredibly gifted at both things," Callum added. It looked like Red wasn't the only one trying to play Cupid tonight.

"What kind of art do you do?"

I was glad he asked about that instead of my novels. Telling him I enjoyed making sculptures out of random garbage was a hell of a lot less embarrassing than fessing up to being an erotica author. While I wasn't ashamed of what I wrote, it seemed like something that might scare him off. "I specialize in found object art."

"Oh, so you mean like sustainable art?"

Damn, he was smart, wasn't he? "Yeah, exactly. I'm impressed. The usual reaction I get is, 'Uh, so is that like a scavenger hunt where you find paintings and shit?' People are so stupid. What school would let you major in scavenger hunts?"

"When I was applying to university, I found some individualized studies programs that would probably let you do that." Callum and Rune had applied to colleges last winter and both would start next month.

Elias tilted his head as he mulled over something. "You know, I bet you could study them. I can imagine a thesis called 'Scavenger Hunts: Legends, Treasures, and the Quest for Hidden Histories on the High Seas in Nineteenth-Century Pirate Literature,' or something like that."

It took a concentrated effort not to crack jokes about pirates plundering booty. Normally, I'd have fun ripping on that, but I wanted Elias to think I was more than just a sex-crazed pervert. I mean, I *was* a sex-crazed pervert, but hopefully by the time he figured that out, he'd be too charmed by me to hate that. "I take it back. That would actually be a pretty cool major."

"It would be neat to combine that with a study on matelotage," Callum said with excitement.

"Mate-what?"

"It's the word that 'mate' derives from. During the seventeenth century, matelotage was a civil union between two male pirates. They would share everything with each other, including women sometimes. Their captain essentially married them, which granted them rights to each other's loot if one of them died. They even exchanged rings."

It was adorable how Callum could never resist geeking out about history. "Are you seriously telling me that pirates pioneered gay marriage, and this is the first I'm hearing about it?"

"Historians insist it was more about the contractual aspect of the arrangement rather than the romantic one, but I'm not sure I believe that. With straight men writing history during a time where homosexuality was punishable by death, the odds they would sanitize the 'unfathomable' romance between male pirates seems high."

"Pirates were lawless marauders who raped, pillaged, looted, and murdered people," Elias said. "Why wouldn't outlaws flagrantly disregard social mores by having sex with each other and falling in love? The gentry would have been aghast at the mere possibility of all that booty plundering happening on pirate ships. I bet it was far more common than we're led to believe."

How did Mr. Shy beat me to the pervy punchline? Making dirty jokes while using fancy words like "gentry" was officially my new favorite thing. It made Elias even more attractive to me. I wanted to get naked and have him talk smart to me while we fucked. My mental image of us together caused me to shift uncomfortably as I struggled against my arousal. "I'm totally looking this up later and writing a story about it." One with lots and lots of hot sex in it, but I kept that to myself. "Maybe about a captain and his cabin boy. Ooh, or better yet, two rival captains. I love a good enemies-to-lovers scenario."

"But if they were rival captains, that would mean they would both have their own ships," Elias commented. "They couldn't be together without giving up one of their ships."

"Exactly. That would be another source of drama for them. It would totally work. I can see it now: one of them conducting a raid on the other captain's ship would lead to confronting him in his quarters. They'd argue with each other until one has his back pressed up against a wall and then start angrily making out. It would be super sexy." My fingers itched to jot the plot bunny down on my phone.

Elias seemed taken aback by my idea, which made me regret not keeping my thoughts inside my head. I was born without a filter, so I forgot to keep my mouth shut sometimes.

He cleared his throat as he tried to be polite about my writing. "Do you often write those kinds of stories?"

"I write contemporary, but the rest of it is pretty much my brand." Not wanting to lose him to that, I attempted to redirect his attention. "I do fantasy stuff in my art, though. I just finished making a dragon out of those pull tabs off soda cans."

"I'd love to see it if you have pictures of it."

Taking out my phone, I pulled up the photos of my latest creation before passing it over to Elias and Callum. "I made a wire frame first, then added the painted tabs. It took me a few months, but I'm pleased with how it came out."

They both exclaimed in surprise, which gratified my ego. I loved the awe in Elias's voice as he said, "This is magnificent! It looks massive."

"Gary's about five feet long by four feet wide."

One of Elias's eyebrows quirked up as he looked at me with a hint of a grin. "Gary the Dragon?"

"Being made of pull tabs, he's not pretentious like *some* dragons who insist on being called Hyrexion or something absurd like that."

Elias's laughter was delightful and made me tingle all over, especially when I noticed how the corners of his eyes crinkled adorably in his amusement. "Fair enough. Well, he may not be pretentious, but he certainly is beautiful."

"I agree. Gary is quite grand," Callum said, giving my phone back to me. "Oh! Elias, you should show him Avery!"

I had no clue who Avery was, but it piqued my curiosity. "Who's that?"

"He's the Kiwi bird who sits on my desk at work and keeps me company." Elias scrolled through his photo album, before handing his phone over to me.

On the screen was the cutest sculpture I had ever seen. It was of a three-inch-tall, rotund bird made of iridescent blue shards, with gold feet and beak. The large black eyes were extra adorable. "Wow, he's *way* cuter than Gary. Did you make this?"

"No, my mom did when I started working for Rhys. Birds are my favorite animal, so she wanted me to have one to keep me company at the office. I have a bigger hummingbird version hanging in my apartment."

I zoomed in on the picture, admiring the magnificent colors of the shattered shards comprising the feathers of the bird. "What's he made of? Broken CDs?"

"Yeah, after Mom digitized her CD collection, she had fun smashing them up to make different sculptures. She also made a family of three birds for the house, a rat for my dad's office as a joke, and an amazing guitar."

I returned his phone. "I'd love to pick her brain sometime about how she makes those. That's stunning."

The light in his eyes dimmed, making me regret my words. "Um, unfortunately, she passed away earlier this year."

"I'm so sorry to hear that."

Callum rested his hand on Elias's arm in silent support.

"She would have enjoyed talking with you, especially about Gary." Watching Elias struggling with his emotions made my heart break for him. He wiped away an unshed tear. "Sorry, I didn't mean to be such a downer. It's just—we were really close, so it's still hard sometimes."

I hated that the booth table was so wide I couldn't reach out and touch him. "You never have to apologize for that. Your mom sounded like an awesome person. I'm close enough to my mom that I've been called a mama's boy by more than one asshole before, so I get it."

"Thanks." He took a deep breath, squaring his shoulders as he rallied himself. "I'd like to see more of your art sometime."

"You're welcome to see it anytime." I'd do damn near anything to spend more time with Elias. I had never felt so certain about needing someone, but I lived my life by trusting my instincts. If they were telling me I had to have him, I was going to do whatever was necessary to make him mine.

A smile tugged at the corner of his mouth, which may as well have been pulling directly on my heartstrings. "Maybe someday I'll be brave enough to read one of your stories."

I couldn't stop myself from smirking. "Who knows? It might even give you an idea or two."

"About what?"

Falling back once more on the mysterious stranger aura, I gave him my most enigmatic expression. It apparently worked, because his cheeks grew bright red as he started laughing. The sound of his amusement made me feel all warm and gooey. What was it about him that turned my insides into a hot brownie? If I got lucky, maybe he would want a bite. And if I was *really* lucky, he'd want to come back for seconds, thirds, fourths, and forever.

Chapter Three

ELIAS

A KNOCK on my office door distracted me from the contract I was reviewing for Rhys's latest project. To my surprise, it was my father, who worked as the lead counsel of our in-house legal team.

We had always had a strained relationship when I was growing up, because he spent more time at the office than he ever did at home. It was part of why I had been so close to my mother; he was never around. Whenever he was with us, his mind had still been focused on work.

But losing Mom had changed him and our dynamic. It had been a bumpy transition as he took a more active role in my life, but it meant a lot to me since he was making a genuine effort to be there for me now that she couldn't be. When I lost her, I was convinced I'd be all alone in the world, but Dad had stepped up when I needed him the most. It helped soothe a lot of my old hurts with our previously distant relationship.

"Hey, do you have a minute?"

"Of course." I gestured for him to come in and take a seat.

He shut the door for privacy before sitting across from me. Mom used to tease him, saying he looked like the stock photo model for an executive with his crisp suit, salt-and-pepper hair, and handsome face. There were at least two paralegals who were aiming to be my new stepmother, but his dedication to the job made him oblivious to their flirting behavior. It was probably for the best. "How's your day been so far?"

It wasn't like Dad to pop in for a brief chitchat. "Pretty good. How's yours?"

"Good, good." He rubbed the back of his hand, which was a nervous tic we both did whenever we got worried. My anxiety spiked, but I tried to keep a lid on it until he told me what was going on. "I wanted to talk to you about something."

Nothing good ever followed that sentence. "Is everything okay?"

"Yeah, I wanted to ask about Friday."

I wracked my brain trying to remember what was happening Friday. "Oh, right. That's when the Laris acquisition goes through. Everything will be ready in time to move forward, no worries."

He gave me a funny look that seemed a little sad. "I'm glad to hear it, but that wasn't what I meant."

"Am I forgetting something?" It was highly possible. After meeting North last Friday, I hadn't been able to get the mysterious man off my mind. I never expected to still be distracted by him three days later.

"Your birthday."

I did a double take as I checked my calendar, blinking at it in disbelief. Wait, how was it almost August twenty-seventh? Wasn't it August sixth like a week ago? My computer said today was the twenty-third, but I couldn't believe that was true. "Oh. Huh, it really snuck up on me this year."

My father chuckled, but the way he rubbed his knuckles betrayed his anxiety. "I hoped maybe you wouldn't mind coming over for dinner so we could celebrate."

That shocked me even more than realizing my birthday was so close. It had always been a day for me and Mom because Dad was so busy with his late nights at the office. That was probably why I had blocked the date from my mind; celebrating without her for the first time wouldn't be much of a celebration.

When I didn't reply, Dad hopefully asked, "I'm sure you have plans with Callum for Friday night, but maybe you could stop by sometime over the weekend?"

"Friday night would be great, Dad. I'd like to spend my birthday with you."

The joy my answer brought to my father's face

was heartwarming. It made me realize how hard he was trying to be a good father. After spending most of my life assuming he didn't care about me or Mom, it was touching to see he genuinely loved me, even if he hadn't always been the best with showing it. "I'm glad. In that case, I'll leave at four so I can have dinner ready for you when you come over after work. How does Tuscan butter gnocchi and creamy chicken sound?"

Him leaving the office early was a gift all by itself. It was further proof of his efforts to repair our relationship. "I'm getting hungry thinking about it. It's one of my favorites."

Dad beamed at the praise. Before Mom passed, he rarely cooked, but when he did, it was always delicious. I had been doing my part to have dinner with him at least once a week. The thought of him alone in their house was too depressing. "Well, I should let you get back to what you were doing."

"Thanks for stopping by. I'm really looking forward to Friday now."

"Me too."

After a few more parting words, he left to go take care of business.

I looked over at Avery, the cute Kiwi bird my mom had made for me out of shards of CDs. It was silly, but sometimes I liked talking to him. I pet the top of his head as I softly asked, "Dad's trying hard, isn't he?"

It was a shame it had taken losing Mom to bring us together, but I was still grateful we had the chance to be there for each other now. We couldn't change our past, but at least we were trying to build a new future as father and son.

Another knock on my open door made me glance up, happy to see it was Callum. He wore an unusually bold eggplant-colored suit, with a teal shirt and purple bow tie. "Wow, what a fantastic suit."

He flushed at the compliment as he sat where my dad had been earlier. "You don't think it's too much?"

"No, you look amazing in it." That was an understatement. The suit was tailored to accentuate all his lines.

"Rune got it for me as a gift, but I worried it was too fancy to wear to work. It's a bit loud for me, but I love it."

"I'm confident you could come in wearing a fuchsia suit and everyone would love it."

Callum grinned. "It's funny you say that, because I tried one on once. I loved it, but I'm not quite that daring yet."

"I don't know why. You have three bow ties that would match it perfectly."

"Oh, at least." His bow tie collection was legendary around the office. "Speaking of Rune, I was wondering if you'd like to come over to our place for dinner to celebrate your birthday? He found an amazing honey garlic glazed salmon recipe I think you'd enjoy."

As someone who hadn't grown up with many close friends, it amazed me Callum remembered my birthday—especially when I had almost forgotten it myself. "That sounds incredible. Would it be okay if I came over this weekend instead of on Friday? I'm visiting Dad then."

Callum was such a kind soul that he radiated happiness over hearing I was celebrating with my father. "Oh, I'm so happy to hear you'll be spending your birthday with him. Saturday is good for us, too."

"Saturday it is, then. What time should I come over?"

"Does six o'clock work for you?"

I nodded. "That sounds perfect."

Callum's expression became playful. "If you wanted to, you could invite North to join us."

After thinking about him so much over the weekend, it was hard not to pounce on the opportunity. But I showed restraint. "I wouldn't want to impose."

"Consider it part of our gift to you."

"But the dinner is already more than enough!" Asking for anything more would be selfish. But I really, really wanted to be selfish for once. I hadn't been brave enough to ask for North's contact info last Friday, so I had no way of getting ahold of him otherwise.

"What if I told you he wanted to see you as much as you want to see him?"

"I'd find that hard to believe. He's an adventurous free spirit, who probably thinks I'm a weird, old nerd."

Callum pointed out the flaws in my argument. "He's friends with me, and I'm by far the geekiest amongst all of us. And you're not *that* much older than him. He's twenty-two."

"Four years can make a big difference sometimes."

"If I can manage a ten-year difference with Rune, four years is nothing," Callum said. "North may seem immature, but he's always serious when he needs to be. He's there for you, no matter what, and is too honest to play games or betray you like Josh did."

The latter part of Callum's words reminded me of my horoscope from that morning. *Don't let your past hold you back anymore, Virgo. Just because things didn't work out before, doesn't mean the same will be true this time. Now's your chance to leave everything in the past where it belongs and take your first steps into a brighter future.*

They both were right. I was letting my fear of another disastrous relationship like Josh stop me from entertaining the notion of North as a romantic partner. Even if he wasn't interested in me that way, at least I would have a new friend. After all, one dinner together didn't automatically make us boyfriends. It would simply be another opportunity to get to know him better. There was nothing wrong with that.

Swallowing down my nerves, I forced myself to take the risk. "If it's not too much trouble, I'd enjoy it if he could join us."

Callum beamed with sunshine and happiness. "Oh, this will be grand! I promise, we'll all have a wonderful time together. Do you have a sticky note and a pen?" I passed both over to him. He pulled out his phone and then wrote a number off his screen in neat print. "Here, this is North's contact info, so you can text him about coming over on Saturday."

"Thanks, I appreciate it." I studied the paper for a moment, feeling a flutter of butterflies inside me at the prospect of reaching out to him unsolicited. What if I had read the situation wrong and he didn't want to hear from me? It was easy to give in to my doubts, but I reminded myself Callum was too kind to encourage me to do something he thought would end in failure. "Are you really okay with this?"

Rather than answer my question directly, he said, "When I first met North, the word that came to mind was 'muchness,' from *Alice in Wonderland*. He's a lot to take in, you know?"

I nodded in agreement. It was definitely a fair way to describe him.

"All of his stories are so wild; you can hardly believe he's telling the truth. But then you meet his sister and his mom and realize he's not lying. He's just led an extraordinarily weird life. But that's what makes him so great, because his strange experiences help him understand things about you that you'd never expect. It's also why he's an incredible author."

"His stories do edge toward the unbelievable sometimes. I mean, his name alone is pretty out-there."

"The first time we met, I made him show me his ID, because I didn't believe him when he told me." We both laughed before Callum continued. "My initial impression was he was a fun, out-there guy, who was far more open about his desires than I was accustomed to. Honestly, I still blush whenever he mentions certain things sometimes."

I had done the same thing several times throughout our dinner. But there was something remarkable about how freely he could talk about sex and never seemed to second-guess himself. After being with Josh, who lied to me from the moment he approached me, North's honesty was one of his biggest appeals. "He certainly isn't afraid to say what's on his mind."

"Felix claims North has never had a thought he didn't share. But there's more to him than that." Callum turned serious. "I was a nervous wreck when I was hired here. This was my first job ever, and I was terrified I would screw up, get fired, lose my visa, and have to go back to Ireland."

Callum had told me about how his dad had kicked him out of the house and disowned him for being gay. Going home would have been putting himself back in that dangerous situation. I could only imagine the fear he must have felt at the idea that everything might be taken away from him in an instant over one mistake. "Thankfully, you don't work for people who would ever do that to you."

"I understand that now, but back then, my fears got the better of me. The rest of the guys, Brody, and Augie, they all reassured me everything would be fine and gave me pep talks I was too scared to believe in. North was the only one who didn't promise me it would all be okay. Instead, he challenged my anxiety."

"I'm not sure I know what you mean."

"North sat me down and asked me what the worst-case scenario was," Callum explained. "He questioned if I really thought my brother would be friends with someone who would fire me after one mistake and send me back to Da. And of course, Brody would never have a friend like that. North then played devil's advocate by saying what if Rhys *was* that kind of jerk. Did I seriously think Brody would let me get sent back to Da without putting up a fight? I know without a doubt he would do anything for me. He would move Heaven and Hell if that was what it took to keep me safe here with him and Augie."

I had always admired the close relationship Callum had with his older brother. As an only child, I was envious of their bond. "He absolutely would."

"And logically, I know that. But all of my doubts made me forget. By asking me those kinds of questions, North forced me to argue against my panic, to prove none of my fears were realistic."

I couldn't help but be impressed. "That's actually a very helpful way of handling that kind of situation."

Callum nodded in agreement. "He didn't dismiss my concerns and give me the same platitudes everyone else did. Instead, he helped me talk everything out until I realized for myself that I would be okay no matter what. That did more for me than being told 'You'll be fine, stop worrying' a hundred times."

Hearing that only made North even more intriguing to me. "Huh, I wouldn't have expected someone as confident and outgoing as him to be that good with addressing anxiety. He seems like he doesn't fear anything in the world."

"There's a lot more to him than his sharp wit and dirty jokes. That side of him is fun to hang out with, but his deeper, more introspective nature makes him a good friend."

If my curiosity hadn't been piqued before, it was now. "I'll text him tonight after work."

"Whatever happens, you both have my blessing."

It was a relief to hear. "I appreciate that."

"For what it's worth, I think you'd both be good for each other."

"How so?"

Callum paused as he considered the best way to phrase his words. "He would bring some more joy into your life, and you would offer him the stability he secretly craves. Everyone likes the fun guy at parties, but very few people see the more serious side of him that wants true love and not just a good time."

His latter comment made me wonder about something else. "Out of curiosity, have you ever read anything he's written?"

"I have," Callum replied, a slight pink tinging his cheeks. "His books are very explicit, but his novels aren't sex for the sake of sex. He dismissively claims it's only about 'people wanting to bone,' but you can tell his characters are yearning to find understanding through their sexual connection. He would disagree with me saying he writes romance, but I'm hoping one day he'll see what I do. Maybe you'll be the person who helps him realize that he's writing love stories."

"Maybe." The thought made me feel more excited than I had any right to be.

Callum touched his cheeks to check if they were as flushed as they felt. "Anyway, I should get back to work. Let me know what North says about joining us on Saturday."

"I could write you a thousand thank-you cards, and it would never be enough for what you've done for me." Getting to become such close friends with Callum was by far the best part of breaking up with Josh, next to never having to see the jerk again.

"That's what friends are for," he said with a beautiful smile before taking his leave.

Left alone with Avery, I picked up North's number and looked at it. "Should I text him?" He didn't reply with words, but I still felt the answer in my bones. "Yeah, I think so, too."

My horoscope was right. I was done letting my past hold me back from my future happiness. Even though it filled me with nervous anticipation, I wanted to take a chance on North.

Chapter Four

NORTH

IT WAS hard to get work done when all I could think about was Elias. When I normally forgot about a guy as soon as someone hotter showed up, it was strange he had been the only thing on my mind for three straight days. I could understand if I was obsessing about hooking up with him the whole time, but I kept wondering about weird shit like what was his favorite way to cuddle. Would he prefer in bed after sex or on the couch while watching a movie? What was it about him that made canoodling a top priority on my list of things I needed to do?

Spending one dinner together did not merit questioning if his hair was as soft as it looked and wishing I could run my fingers through it to find out. When I fantasized about guys, it was all about getting myself off, not imagining how satisfying it would feel to make him moan as I pleasured him. How had he rewired my dumbass brain in a single meeting?

"Okay, what the fuck is going on with you, North?"

I glanced over at my sexy roommate, Felix. From the moment we met, I had been insanely attracted to him, his slender hips, his gorgeous gray-green eyes, his tight ass, his handsome face, and smart mouth. But I had desperately needed a new roommate to help split the rent more than a live-in fuck buddy, so I behaved myself. It was a challenge to do, especially when his hair was damp from his shower. With his cheeks still flushed, he had the same satiated glow that a good fuck would give. Normally, it made me hide my hard-on under my laptop, but it did nothing for me now. What was wrong with me?

When Felix arched an eyebrow at me in silent question, I realized I hadn't answered him. Try as I might, I had been too distracted to remember what he had asked. "Huh?"

"You're seriously worrying me."

"What? Why?"

Felix closed his laptop to give me his full attention. "You're over there sighing like a lovelorn Victorian lady awaiting a letter from her beloved or something. What's going on?"

His description made me laugh, although it was a little too on the nose for my tastes when that was exactly how I felt. Setting aside my computer, I held in another sigh. "I can't stop thinking about a guy."

He snorted at my comment. "And this differs from any other day how?"

It was a fair point when I was notorious for being man crazed. "I like this one."

"Again, how is this any different from normal?"

"Because it's not just I'd like to fuck him. I *like* him."

My confession made Felix take my situation more seriously. "You mean like him in the sense of wishing you were his boyfriend and not having a one-night stand?"

It sounded so unbelievable when he put it that way. "It's super weird, right?"

"I'd say. I didn't think there was a man alive who would make you pine to be with them as a partner rather than an easy lay."

"I know, right?" How had Elias made me want something I never considered important before? "What's wrong with me?"

Felix stretched out his long legs on the coffee table. That would usually make me think about him wrapping them around my waist as I fucked him but not now. "It's normal to like someone that way."

"Sure, for other people. For me, it's downright bizarre that I want to hold him, and hear about his day, and make him laugh, and—"

"Shit, you actually like him?"

I ruffled my hair with an irritated huff. "Yeah, and it sucks."

"Why?"

"Because he's an adult."

Felix laughed. "*You're* an adult."

"Not like him. He's got his shit together. I make sculptures out of garbage and write smut, and he's an attorney. I'm nowhere close to being worthy of him. Why would he ever waste time with me? I wouldn't if I were him."

"Wow, this is the first time I've seen you be anything less than confident and self-assured." Felix gave me a sympathetic look. "I can't believe I have to say this to you, but you're not giving yourself enough credit here. You're hot as hell and fun to hang out with. There's a lot of appeal in that, especially if he's surrounded by other stuffy lawyers."

I shrugged, still not convinced. "He seemed overwhelmed by me."

"In fairness, everyone's overwhelmed by you at first, me included," Felix said with a fond laugh. "It's not news that you're a lot to handle sometimes."

"I should come with a warning label."

"Only one?"

I had to laugh at that. "I'm sure you're right. Elias probably—"

"Elias? Wait, are you talking about Callum's attorney friend from work?"

"Yeah. Do you know him, too?"

"Callum forgot something at my brother's place a month ago, so I offered to take it to him at the office since it was on my way here. When I dropped it off, he introduced me to Elias." Felix's grin was wicked sexy. "Wow, this makes a *lot* more sense now."

Things may have become clearer for him, but I was lost. "How so?"

"He's super cute," Felix said, making an ugly jealousy I had no right to feel flare through me. "Elias is the shy, adorkable type, which is the complete antithesis of all the bros you bang normally. You have no idea how to handle him."

My ego bristled a bit at the implied slight. "If I could get him into bed, I could handle him just fine, thank you very much."

"Oh, I don't doubt about your ability to show him a great time. That's not what I'm talking about, though." His laugh helped soothe my irritation. "You're used to walking up to a guy at a frat party and going, 'Hey, you're sexy; I'm hot. Wanna fuck?' That shit won't fly with Elias, who would turn into an embarrassed, blushing cherry if you tried that move on him. Guys like him don't fuck; they make love."

I lay down on the couch with a groan. "I know, and it blows. He deserves romance, which means some other guy gets to be the lucky bastard who ends up with him and not me."

"Dude, you literally write romance novels. If you can't romance him, who the hell can?"

"No, I write erotica. I deal purely in the realm of the physical, and he has emotional needs I don't know how to meet."

Felix scoffed at my feeble protest. "You keep saying that, but I'm not buying it. Yes, your work has a lot of sex in it, but that doesn't automatically mean they're erotica. You have plots and genuine emotions between the characters, which gives the cerebral sex more meaning."

"*Cerebral* sex?" I cracked up at the description. "What the hell is that?"

"It means your characters aren't connecting solely on an 'insert Tab A into Slot B, smash until they come' kind of level," Felix explained. "Your story about the student and his professor was as much about their intellectual attraction as their physical one. You're a talented enough author that their sex mirrors that deeper mental connection. It went far beyond 'Hey, you're hot, I'm into taboo shit, let's go fuck in an empty classroom.' Why do you keep trying to downplay your own work?"

I said the same thing I always said. "It's just sex."

"No, mindlessly fucking with frat boys whose name you'll forget in the morning is just sex. Being with someone like Elias is about more than that. You'll find that same connection with him that your characters do in your stories. Quit pining away for him, and take action like you always do with everything else."

Felix made it sound so easy. "He didn't give me his contact info, and I can't ask Callum for it. He'd think I'd only want to hook up with Elias for a quick fuck."

"Or, you could tell him you're serious about Elias and want to date him for real."

The thought of Elias being my boyfriend made my stomach do flips. It was something I had never been interested in before, but with him, it was all I wanted. "What if I'm not boyfriend material?"

"If you want him bad enough, you'll learn how to be the perfect boyfriend for him," Felix predicted. I hoped he was right.

Before I could say anything, I jolted when my phone buzzed in my pocket with an alert. I sat up to fish it out, then stared at the screen in disbelief. The notification badge had a text from an unknown number.

> ELIAS
>
> Hi, I'm sorry to bother you so late. This is Elias Forthwright from the other night. Callum gave me your number, so I hope it's okay that I reached out to you.

A bomb of joy detonated in my heart that Elias had taken the initiative to contact me first. Bless Callum for giving him my info. I guess I made a better impression as the mysterious stranger than I thought.

"Is that good shock or bad shock?" Felix asked.

"Good shock. Elias texted me to say hi." A thrill ran through me at saying it out loud.

"That's great! Don't be stupid and play a waiting game with him because you're afraid of looking too eager to answer him back."

Before Felix had finished his sentence, I had already replied to Elias. There wasn't a chance in hell I was going to play a "make him wait a few days so I don't look desperate" game. I *was* desperate to talk to him. It was all I had been dreaming about doing for three damn days. I refused to wait a second longer than I had to. He seemed too mature to play that kind of head game, anyway. "I answered him."

"Good. Now you can stop sighing dramatically every two seconds because you want to see him again." Felix picked his computer back up and opened it. "For what it's worth, I'm thrilled you've finally found someone who's made you think with your heart for once and not just your dick."

"You and me both."

If I thought I had been happy to hear from Elias before, it was nothing compared to my excitement when I read his next message.

> **ELIAS**
>
> I know this is a bit sudden, but are you free Saturday night? Callum and Rune invited me over to their place for my birthday. I'd really like you to join us if you're interested.

> Should I bring a present?

> You joining us is already part of the present. Besides, my actual birthday is on Friday.

I should have guessed his birthday would be soon since he was a Virgo. It was like another gift from the cosmic universe, one which I was all too happy to accept.

> A two-day celebration? I like the way you party.

ELIAS

> It won't be a party per se. Friday night is just dinner with my dad, then another dinner with Callum, Rune, and you on Saturday.

When I found his literalness adorable, I knew I was in too deep. But I was soaring high that he wanted to invite me and only me to join them.

> I can't wait to celebrate with you.

ELIAS

> I'm looking forward to seeing you again, too.

"Your face is going to split in half if your grin gets any bigger," Felix teased me.

"That's because he invited me to celebrate his

birthday with him this weekend." Was it possible that he had also spent the last three days wishing to spend more time with me? Since when was I that lucky? "He said he's looking forward to seeing me again, too. Do you think that means he asked Callum for my number today?"

"Probably. Wow, I'm impressed. I never thought I'd see the day a sweetheart tamed you."

"Neither did I."

We shared a laugh as we both got back to work on our computers. The warm glow inside of me at knowing I'd be spending time with Elias again soon made everything a million times better. If I played my cards right, maybe I could meet him a little earlier than expected.

Chapter Five

ELIAS

IT WAS strange how you could be both happy and sad at the same time. Spending my birthday with my dad had been a lot more fun than I had expected. Despite that, I couldn't escape the oppressive absence of my mom, who had never missed one before. I did my best not to focus on it, but it was challenging when my eyes kept straying to her empty seat at the kitchen table.

"Dad, dinner was excellent tonight. I'm not sure what was different, but it tasted even better than usual."

It was cute how pleased he was by the praise. Out of his work suit and dressed in casual clothes, he looked much younger when he wasn't the stern businessman at the office. "I saw on one of my cooking shows that they used a different combination of spices for their chicken, so I thought I'd give that a try. It turned out pretty good, didn't it?"

"Better than good. It was fantastic." Dad had gotten into reality cooking shows as a way of passing time when he was home alone. He had started incorporating some techniques he saw the contestants use, with delicious results. "Thanks for making my birthday dinner so special."

"I'm glad you enjoyed it, son." Dad got up and went over to open the bread garage, which was a thing that amused me. It was a door built into the kitchen cabinets that could be lifted up where my parents kept their bread. To my surprise, he pulled out a small box and brought it over to me. "I also got you a little something."

"Oh, you didn't have to do that."

He sat down and passed me the present. "I know I didn't have to, but I wanted to. After the year you've had, you deserved something nice. It's not much, but I thought you'd like it."

The gift was covered in metallic blue wrapping paper. My mom had been a master at wrapping presents with origami techniques and hidden tape that made people want to save the paper afterward to show their friends. Since she was always in charge of gift wrap, I had never seen my dad wrap anything in my life. I had assumed he hadn't known how to do it. He had done his best to wrap the rounded box, using way too much tape. It was clumsily done, but he had tried his best instead of having a store take care of it.

He even remembered to use paper that was my favorite color. It meant a lot.

I carefully tore off the paper, then opened the box. Inside was a beautiful watch, with silver trim and a black leather band. The bezel was a rounded hexagon, with stylized silver numbers on a black face that kept it from being too understated. It perfectly aligned with my aesthetic and was thoughtful, since watches was one of the common interests Dad and I shared. "Wow, it's so beautiful! This is perfect. Thank you." Smart watches were great, but nothing beat a beautiful timepiece for me.

"I'm glad you like it. I thought it was a nice balance between having some flare while still being classical."

It was yet another reminder that my father knew me better than I previously gave him credit for. I took off my watch and put on the new one, admiring how it looked. "It's the perfect size for my bird bones, too." I had slender wrists, so normal men's watches were comically absurd on me because they were so big. "I love it. Thank you, Dad."

He smiled at me with fatherly pride. "I'm glad. This past year has taught me that there's never enough time, so I want to be better about treasuring moments like these. I can't make up for all the years I wasn't around, but I'm doing my best now to be the dad I should have been all along."

It was true he had rarely been around while I was growing up, but I hadn't resented it because Mom and I had been so close. That was why after she passed, I assumed I'd be all alone in the world. At first, that was exactly how things had turned out as Dad threw himself deeper into his work out of grief. But after my breakup with Josh, Dad attempted to be there for me in a way he never had been before. I could have been mad that it took Mom dying for him to do that, but after losing her, I'd rather focus on the effort he was making to be an active part of my life now. "And I appreciate that. I'm grateful that we've been able to grow closer."

Dad rubbed the back of his hand as he smiled sadly. "I'm sorry it took losing your mom to make me realize how much time I lost with you both. I got so fixated on giving you both a better life than the one I had, I forgot to be part of the family I was trying so hard to support. I'm so thankful that you had such a wonderful and loving mother, because I was a lousy excuse for a father."

"I don't feel that way at all. There's nothing wrong with wanting to give your family a good life."

It broke my heart to see the guilt eating away at him. "Like your mom, you try to make things better for people, even for someone like me who doesn't deserve it."

While I understood where his concerns were coming from, I needed Dad to know that I didn't feel that way. It made my decision easier as I got up to go over to where I had left my bag earlier. I had been carrying around something to give to him for a while, but I had never worked up the nerve before. It was time to change that.

I pulled it out and brought it back over to the table for Dad. "Here."

He looked puzzled. "What's that?"

"Proof that I don't hold the past against you."

He accepted the small white envelope. I tried not to let my nervousness show as he opened my thank-you note and read it out loud. "I know we haven't always been close. But over these past few months, I've enjoyed getting to spend so much time with you and learning about who you really are. I don't know how I would have gotten through this without your love and support. I'm grateful every day—" My dad's voice cracked with emotions. He cleared his throat before continuing. "I'm grateful every day that we can be there for each other. Thank you for being the amazing father I needed to help me get through this past year. I love you, Dad."

Both of us were emotional by the time he finished reading my note. I leaned over to embrace him, hiding that I was almost in tears over seeing how moved he was by my words. He gave me a tight bear hug. "I love you, too, son. I'm so proud of the man you've become. I hope you know that."

"I do." When I pulled back, we both had to wipe away the tears that had gathered in the corner of our eyes. "I meant every word of my note. I really am lucky to have you as my dad."

It was rare to see my father being so emotional. "I know thank-you cards were you and your mom's thing. It meant the world to her when you would write her one every day after she got sick. They helped get her through some of her toughest moments. I was happy that you took the time to let her know how much you loved and appreciated her and all that she had done for you. Deep in my heart of hearts, I knew I hadn't done anything to deserve one of your cards. I never thought I'd be a good enough father for that."

"But you have been," I insisted. "You were right before about there never being enough time. That's why I don't want to waste it on being mad about things that happened in the past we can't change. I'd much rather celebrate that you're trying so hard now to be the best dad you can be. Especially since that dad is the best dad I could have ever asked for."

He got up and gave me a proper hug. I once again had to fight back tears, knowing that our reconciliation was yet another gift from Mom. I still wished that she was with us, but it meant everything to me that Dad loved me and was doing everything he could to make sure I knew it.

When we parted, he tried to lighten the mood. "Should we find out if the cake I baked you wins me the Father of the Year Award?"

"That sounds great." Cake or not, he had already won that prize in my eyes.

MY HOROSCOPE that morning had predicted that I would receive an unexpected gift today. It had come true when Dad gave me a final thing before I left—my mom's last birthday present to me. It was sitting on my kitchen table as I stared at it, trying to sort through my jumble of feelings.

Even when she had been dying, Mom had still had the wherewithal to make sure I had a present for my birthday. It was so typical of her I had to laugh, except it made me feel like crying because she wasn't here to give it to me herself. Most kids received store-bought presents for their birthday, but my mother handmade me a single present each year. The beautiful hummingbird made of shattered CDs hanging in my home office had been her gift to me last year, right before she got diagnosed. She named all her sculptures, and she had chosen Bertie because it was how I used to pronounce "birdie" when I was little. It was also her nickname for me. I'd give almost anything to hear her call me that again.

I was brimming with curiosity over what her last gift would be, but I wasn't sure if I was emotionally prepared to handle the devastation. Logically, I knew it wouldn't be the final thing she gave me. I still had a box of cards she left for me to open on special occasions and for just-because moments when I needed something to brighten my day. But there was a finality to opening it that made it difficult to act.

She had also chosen a blue wrapping paper for me, only hers was holographic and shimmered with light. Her philosophy had always been "the shinier, the better." That was part of the reason she had loved making so many things out of broken shards of CDs. The iridescent reflections that sent cascades of light on the wall made her sculptures even more beautiful.

It was finally too much to bear, so I pulled the box closer to me and carefully unwrapped the present. She had learned how to wrap presents like origami art, hiding the tape under the creased seams of the paper. My grief welled up that I would never again receive such a beautifully wrapped present as I did my best not to rip the paper as I removed it.

Underneath was a beautiful square silver holographic box. I took off the lid, revealing an envelope. One of her quirks was wrapping cards inside the presents, because for her, they were an equally important part of the gift. She always made her own cards, and this one was no exception. It featured an adorable color sketch of Avery, my cute Kiwi bird I kept at work that she'd made me. He was sitting next to a birthday cake, wearing a party hat, while blowing one of those birthday kazoo things. I loved it so much that it took me a few minutes before I could open the card to read her well-wishes.

Bertie,

Happy Birthday, honey! I'm sorry I've made a mess of things by not physically being there, but I'm always there for you in spirit. Except for when you're in the bathroom or need some alone time. Some things should stay private, after all. The last thing you need is me giving you a complex about whether I'm watching you at all times. Although giving your future boyfriend the heebie-jeebies that I might be sneaking a peek could be fun for you down the road. Besides, I have to check in on your father every once in a while, right? What kind of ghost would I be if I didn't do that? I've got to get up to at least a little ooky spooky fun, or I'm pretty sure they'll revoke my haunting license.

I laughed at my mom haunting dad. Most people used that as a threat, but leave it to Mom to think it was an affectionate way to tease us, even in death. It might not be possible, but I liked thinking it was true. It made her feel a little closer to me, which made me less sad.

> *Speaking of your dad, thank you for being such a good son and checking in on him. It would be easy to grow even more distant, but I made you more stubborn than that. He's never been great about showing his emotions, but I promise he loves you more than anything else. If you look close enough, you'll see it in all the little things he does. I'm sure he's started cooking for you, because that's how he shows his love. He may have (sadly) dropped his charming Southern accent, but you can't take the Southern gentleman out of him. He usually goes light on the salt, so if your dish is perfectly seasoned, that's totally me lending a ghostly helping hand by adding an extra pinch of it to perfection when he isn't looking.*

Tonight's dinner actually had been well seasoned, which I attributed to the different spices he mentioned using. It was nice thinking it was because Mom figured out how to astrally manipulate a saltshaker, though.

> I probably owe you and your father an apology for what I had to do to make your gift. There were several noble sacrifices made for it to come into existence. And if I'm being honest, I'm salty about time right now, so smashing the hell out of them was a lot of fun for me. Consider this my way of getting a little head start on being sacrilegious as practice for the afterlife.
>
> I want this to serve as a reminder to show your inner clockwork to the man who will truly love you for the gift that you are. Don't lock yourself away in your grief, Bertie. Let him in to see all the beautiful gears that turn inside you. Is this a heavy-handed metaphor? You bet. But I've had so much fun making this over the past few months, that I'm sure you can forgive me for getting a little carried away with my last masterpiece.
>
> His name is North, because as long as you follow your heart, it'll always lead you

in the right direction. He'll watch over you, love you, and protect you, because that's why he was created. He was made for you. I want you to remember every time you see him that you are loved.

My jaw dropped as I reread that paragraph over again. Then I read it a third and fourth time, just to be sure my eyes weren't deceiving me. Out of all the infinite names my mother could have picked in the universe, how had she decided on choosing *that* name? What were the odds that she would have named her creation after the one man I couldn't stop thinking about? Wow, she really wasn't joking about getting up to some ooky spooky stuff in the afterlife. It sent a cold chill through me.

I love you so much, sweetheart. Please know that I would have done absolutely anything to spend even one more day in person with you. It's not fair, but I guess I'll have to settle for phenomenal cosmic powers as a tradeoff for having to love you from afar. This may be the last physical present I'm able to make for you, but it won't be the final gift I give you.

I've already started planning for stuff to do once I cross over, so prepare yourself. When the man of your dreams shows up when you least expect it, remember to thank your awesome mom for sending you Mr. Right. He won't be who you think he'll be, because you know I love surprises. But I promise he'll be the one who falls in love with you and your beautiful clockwork that makes you tick. If you ever doubt that, North will always be happy to remind you how loved you are.

Even though it defied logic and the odds, I really, really hoped my mom managed to do the impossible and make that happen. If anyone could do it, it'd be her.

Happy birthday, Bertie. Bringing you into this world was by far the best thing I ever did. I'm so proud of you, and I thank my lucky stars every day that I'm allowed to be your mom. I may not be able to stay with you physically as long as I had hoped, but not even death can get rid of me that easily. My love for you is too infinite and strong to let a pesky thing like dying get between us. I'll love you forever and always.

With all the love in this world and the next,

Mom

I held it together long enough to finish reading, but my emotions were getting harder and harder to hold back. Setting aside the card so I didn't make the ink run from crying, I wiped away the tears before they could fall. Mom wouldn't have wanted me to cry, especially not on my birthday, but it was hard when her words made her feel so close yet so far away.

It took some time before I could compose myself enough to open the rest of her present. Another smaller box was wrapped inside, because she loved a grand reveal. Once again, I undid the meticulous wrapping, revealing a holographic gold box. My fingers trembled as I lifted the lid off it.

Nestled on an iridescent Easter grass nest was the most beautiful bird I had ever seen. North was a small sparrow made of recycled watch parts, with a body built from gears and broken movements. The red and blue sapphire jewels that powered watches caught the light, making him sparkle. It looked like a steampunk pet bird, and I could almost see the gears whirling as it flapped its wings. The craftsmanship was exquisite, and I couldn't believe that my mom had built such an intricate sculpture while being ravaged by aggressive pancreatic cancer. It was a testament to her stubbornness that she created something as magnificent as North while fighting for her life.

Hiding my face in my hands, my cries came out as sobs as I lost my battle to my emotions. Everything I had been holding back spilled over as I felt her loss all over again, a deep, never-ending chasm of pain that hurt like hell. I hated that I couldn't talk to her now, that I couldn't tell her about North, thank her for her amazing gift, hug her, or joke with her anymore. Every time I thought I had gotten a handle on my grief, something like this would rip my heart open. I didn't want to be sad about receiving such an incredible present, but the unfairness of losing her so young made it hard not to be bitter sometimes.

I felt like crap by the time my tears had lessened to stuffy sniffles. Wasn't crying supposed to make you feel better? All it did was make my eyes feel like sandpaper and my head stuffed with cotton. I got up to get a drink of water and wash off my face.

As I continued trying to regain my composure, my phone buzzed with an alert. To my surprise, it wasn't a message from Dad.

> **NORTH**
> Are you free?

The hair on the back of my neck raised as I glanced over at the avian clockwork North sitting on my kitchen table.

> Free for what?

> **NORTH**
> A visitor.

> You want to come over to my apartment right now?

> Only if you want me to.

My mother's words from her birthday card came back to me: *"This may be the last physical present I'm able to make for you, but it won't be the final gift I give you."*

Without hesitation, I texted him my address. I then sat down to wait at my kitchen table, studying the intricacies of the gear work on my mom's sculpture. Whatever was going to happen, I was ready for it.

NORTH ARRIVED with a purple box in his hands, which had half a donut in the shape of a crescent moon and the word "Insomnia" emblazoned over it. He once again was wearing jeans and a band T-shirt.

His grin was so bright that I couldn't help but smile back. "Happy birthday!"

"Thanks. Come in." I stepped aside so he could enter my apartment, then led him over to my kitchen table. My excitement surprised me over getting to see him earlier and alone before our dinner with Callum and Rune tomorrow night. "Are those donuts?"

"Yeah, I figured you probably had cake already, so I wanted to switch it up." He set the box on the table and opened it to reveal an incredible assortment of donuts. "I got them from Insomnia Donuts on my way over here, so they're super fresh."

"I've never tried them before, but they look great." I got us napkins since plates seemed too formal for donuts. They all looked so wonderful. It was hard to pick, but I settled for one with rainbow sprinkles on top of white icing. "This was sweet of you."

The surprises kept coming as he pulled out a box of candles and placed one on my donut. I hid my amusement behind my hand as he struggled to get his lighter to work.

"Damn it, people make this look so easy on TV!" He made a triumphant noise when the flint produced a flame, allowing him to light the wick. "There! Make a birthday wish."

Mom, go ahead and work your magic. I want you to be right about North. Wish made, I blew out the candle.

"I bet your wish is going to come true soon."

"Oh?" I pulled the candle out of my donut,

sucking the icing off the bottom before setting it on my napkin. "What makes you so certain of that?"

"Just a feeling. Can I have this one?" I agreed, so he picked a Bavarian cream donut out of the box. He tapped it against mine like we were toasting with drinks. "Cheers."

I chuckled before taking a bite. "Wow, you weren't kidding about these being fresh. This might be the best donut I've ever eaten."

"If you want a taste of heaven, try their glazed ones when they're fresh off the line. They're melt-in-your-mouth good, especially at 3:00 a.m. when you're in the middle of finals week. Speaking of good, how was dinner with your dad?"

It touched me that he remembered my plans I had mentioned earlier in the week. "It went really well. He made a delicious dinner for us, and we spent a wonderful evening talking. We weren't close when I was growing up, so he's trying hard to make up for that now that Mom isn't here anymore."

"I think I kind of know what you mean. My dad travels a lot, so it's always been me, West, and Mom. He'd come home, and it'd feel like a stranger was having dinner with us sometimes. He wasn't a kid kind of guy, so I think he didn't know how to relate to us when we were little. I can't blame him when West and I were a lot to deal with. Now that we're older, he's way better about being with us whenever he is home."

It surprised me North understood where I was coming from on the subject. "I think Dad keeps expecting me to have all this built-up anger and resentment toward him for not being around when I was growing up. But honestly, I'm more appreciative that he came through for me when I needed him the most. It felt great to tell him that tonight."

The way North licked the cream out of his donut flustered me with inappropriate thoughts. "Yeah, I low-key feel like an asshole about being fine with Dad never being around when I was younger, because life was fantastic when it was the three of us without him. It was weirder whenever he was there. But now it's like I have two different dads, so it's weird explaining that to people who don't get it."

That was the same way I felt about my mine. I had been fine with him always being at work, because Mom was there for me and made life fun. "You're right. It's almost like a Before Dad and an After Dad, because the man who is my amazing father now is not the same guy who raised me."

"Or didn't raise you, at least in my case. That was all my mom's doing. Everyone assumed she was a badass single parent when we were kids. I mean, she kind of was when you think about it."

"So was mine."

North gave me a sympathetic look that was mercifully free of pity. "That's probably been hard for you today, hasn't it?"

It was nice to have someone who wasn't my father acknowledge that fact. Callum had been right that North seemed to have an uncanny ability to understand things about me I'd never expect. "Honestly, it's been tough." It was a relief to admit out loud what I had been struggling with all day. "I keep yo-yoing between ignoring that she isn't here, missing her so much, and feeling like she's been here with me all along."

North pointed at the silver holographic box I had left on the kitchen table. "She got you whatever's in there, didn't she?"

When I knew he was on his way over, I had put her present back inside it. It seemed important to see his reaction when he saw her sculpture for the first time. "What makes you say that?"

"Because anybody who creates sculptures out of shiny, shattered CDs is somebody who also loves holographic gift boxes."

It amazed me he didn't know much about my mom, but he had already figured that out about her. I removed the lid and set her card aside, before taking out the smaller gold box to show him. "She lived for shiny things. Nothing could ever be too shiny for her tastes."

"That's my kind of lady," he said with a laugh. "I can't wait to see what's inside."

I watched him as I took off the gold lid. His eyes widened in surprise as he breathed in awe, "*Wow.*" He never looked away as I stood the clockwork bird on the table so he could get a closer glimpse. He got down on eye level with it as he continued marveling at it with wonder. "This is incredible! Your mom is an absolute legend."

My emotions stirred up again by the amazed way he talked about her and referred to her in present tense. Just because Mom wasn't here anymore didn't mean that she stopped being the best at everything. "She really is."

"It's the cutest steampunk bird ever."

"She made him out of watch parts." After seeing him, her comments about being salty over time and taking pleasure from destroying watches made a lot more sense.

He continued studying the sculpture, taking in every detail. "What's his name?"

I took a steadying breath before I answered, "North."

He lifted his gaze to glance up at me. "Yeah?"

"His name is North."

The sexy smile that graced North's lips made my heart dance wildly in my chest. "You named him after me?"

"No, my mom did."

He tilted his head with a puzzled look. "What do you mean? Your mom never met me."

I picked up her birthday card, hesitating for a moment over sharing something so personal. But I steeled my reserve and handed it to him. I needed him to see it.

He took the card out with a curious expression, which became one of delight when he saw her illustration. "Avery! Wow, she could draw, too? I'm so jealous. I can build stuff, but my sketches are nowhere near this good."

It warmed my heart that he had remembered such a minor detail as my bird's name. His genuine appreciation for Mom's art touched me. Once again, I observed him as he opened the card and began to read.

North immediately started laughing. "I don't know which I love more: that your mom is cool enough to want to give you privacy while you get off or that she's down to peep on your sexy boyfriend. Also, 'ooky spooky' is officially my new favorite term ever."

"Her favorite part about Halloween was having a full month where she could use it and not get weird looks."

He grinned at me. "Which means she still used it the other eleven months of the year, but she got some side-eye for it?"

"Exactly."

North continued reading the card with a small smile on his face. That promptly turned into a broad grin when he reached the part where she talked about destroying watches. "Wow, your mom never let anything get her down, did she?"

"She prided herself on being relentlessly optimistic, with emphasis on relentless."

He chuckled, then resumed reading. It was fascinating watching his expression shift into an almost fond smile, before his jaw dropped in disbelief the same as mine had. After rereading the paragraph about why her sculpture was named North, he stared up at me in amazement. "You said your mom was really into horoscopes, right?"

"Yeah. She read them every day."

"Was she also psychic? Because this is way too wild to be a coincidence."

I shrugged, since I didn't have an answer for why she was so eerily accurate in her predictions. "It makes you wonder if she got a head start on gaining those phenomenal cosmic powers she mentioned."

His gaze returned to the card once more, his eyebrows arching in disbelief as he read her next paragraph about sending me Mr. Right when I least expected it. He closed it when he finished, looking at her illustration once more as he took a moment to gather his thoughts. He didn't look at me as he asked, "Which would bother you more: her being right or wrong?"

"I'm not sure I know what you mean."

"Would it upset you if I wanted to watch over you, love you, and protect you like she said? If she was correct about me being the one who falls in love with you and all the things that make you tick, would that be upsetting to you?" When he finally made eye contact with me, my heart raced from the intensity of the moment. "Is there any world where I could be your Mr. Right like she predicted?"

It was a challenge to find my voice. "W-why would that upset me?"

"Because you deserve a man worthy of you, who knows what he wants to do with his life and is successful enough to give you everything you've ever wanted. I'm a dumb college kid who has no idea what he's going to do after he graduates and has nothing to offer you other than my heart. You could do so much better than me."

"But what if you're who I want?" I asked in a soft voice. "Because I've dated the guy who was Mr. Right on paper. He was successful, handsome, and could have given me the life I'm supposed to want. But it was all a lie. He treated me like trash and cheated on me with two other men. I may not have known you for very long, but my instincts tell me you're an honest man."

"I'd rather cut off my own dick than cheat on you." North moved to kneel in front of me, looking up at me with a beseeching gaze that made me want to give him anything he asked for. "From the first moment I saw you in the bar, I haven't been able to stop thinking about you. I've never done the boyfriend thing, and I may be really shitty at it, but everything in me wants your mom to be right about me."

I wanted the same thing, which was why I allowed myself to uncharacteristically give in to my urge to kiss him without overthinking it. When Josh had kissed me, it had been harsh, almost punishing as he aggressively staked his claim on me. But North cupped my face in his hands, caressing my cheeks as he tenderly returned my affection. His gentleness melted away any lingering reservations I may have had about whether I was making the right decision. For a day I had expected to be marred by my heavy sadness, I had never felt happier than I did in that very moment. Being with North was a gift I was more than willing to accept with the utmost gratitude.

Thanks for not making me wait for my birthday wish to come true, Mom. I swore I could almost hear her giggling with glee. That was fine with me. She deserved a good laugh after pulling off a miracle.

Chapter Six

NORTH

I HAD KISSED a lot of men in my life. Because I liked an easy lay with whoever was hot and down to fuck, most of my kisses had been of the sloppy drunk, overeager with too much tongue, or devouring each other's mouths as we ripped off our clothes kinds of kisses. There was rarely any finesse involved because my partners were more interested in the fucking part than making out. Given the choice between a tongue tango or a blow job, I would choose the latter every time.

But being kissed by Elias was a new experience for me. Instead of being a promise of sex in my immediate future, it was a whispered confession of his heart's feelings. It made mine overflow with a rush of intense emotions I had never felt for anyone before. I had always thought instant love was Hollywood bullshit, but a single kiss was all it took for me to fall stupid in love with him. It was such a pure feeling that not even someone as dirty-minded as me could make it perverse.

When he drew back, his bashful expression was too precious for words. To my great relief, there wasn't a shadow of regret in his gorgeous gray eyes, only a slight shyness about being so bold.

I wrapped my arms around his waist and pulled him closer to me. Kneeling between his legs made my mouth practically water from how badly I wanted to suck his dick, but there would be plenty of time for that later. Instead, I looked up at him and couldn't resist teasing him. "See? I told you your birthday wish would come true soon."

"What makes you think you were my birthday wish?"

"A little birdie told me."

I loved the sound of his delighted laughter and the way it almost seemed to make light dance in his eyes. "I guess it had to be the little one since you haven't met the bigger one yet."

"Can I?"

"Sure." He led me through his impeccably decorated apartment to his office. When he turned on the lights, I noticed the remarkable hummingbird sculpture hanging from the ceiling. Like Avery, he was made from CD shards, with gold claws and a beak. His large wings were spread wide, like he was swooping in on a flower. The blue, purple, and pink iridescent reflective finish on the discs cast scattered fractals on the wall. It was a stunning work of art that I got as close as I dared to study it.

I had never worked with CDs before, but something told me it wasn't nearly as easy as his mom made it appear. She was such an incredible artist, and I wished I could learn from her. If I was bummed about not being able to meet someone so awesome, I could only imagine the hellish grief Elias must feel over losing such an amazing mother. It would fuck me up if I lost my mom at any age, let alone so young. "He's magnificent. What's his name?"

"Bertie. That was Mom's nickname for me since I was a kid, because whenever I tried to say 'birdie,' it always came out as 'bertie' instead. She gave him to me when I moved in here a few years ago."

"Well, both bird Bertie and boy Bertie are adorable." When I glanced over at him, he had a small smile on his face, but traces of sadness lingered as he gazed at the sculpture. I took advantage of the fact that we were both standing to give him a proper hug. "Thank you for letting me come over tonight to celebrate with you and see your mom's amazing art."

He hugged me back, burying his face against my neck as I stroked his white-blond hair. It was even softer than I had imagined it would be. "I'm glad you're here."

That made me happy to hear, because it meant I wouldn't be leaving anytime soon, hopefully. "What do you say to staying up late and getting to know each other a little better?"

Elias pulled back to look at me but didn't step out of my embrace. "Do you mean we should, um…"

It was cute the way he trailed off with a blush. While my dick was very much interested in hearing him finish his sentence, for once, I wanted to get to know him by talking instead of carnally. "How does curling up on the couch as we ask each other a million questions sound?"

His smile was so radiant that I basked in it like the warmth of the sun. "That would be nice."

"Good, because I'm dying to know if you prefer hard or squishy cookies." My heart fluttered like hummingbird wings when he took my hand to lead me into his living room.

"That's your number one question for me?" he asked with a laugh.

We sat on his navy blue couch together. The area was elegant, while still being comfortable. "If your answer isn't both, we're going to be off to a rocky start."

He rubbed the back of his left hand as he timidly asked, "For the Q&A or for dating?"

I stretched my arm out to wrap around his shoulders and draw him closer to me. "Sorry, it was a bad joke. You could hate cookies and I'd still be thanking my lucky stars that I get to be your boyfriend."

His radiant smile lit me up inside. Shit, I had it

bad for him already, and we were only getting started. I hoped he was prepared for me to love him more than I had loved anything else ever. His cuteness was too much to take, so I leaned in to steal a lingering kiss. It was so tempting to delve in for a taste of him, but I restrained myself to sucking on his lower lip before I released him.

"For the record, I prefer soft cookies over hard, but I love them both," he answered.

"You really are the perfect boyfriend for me."

He chuckled at my reaction. "It doesn't take much to impress you, does it?"

"All you have to do to wow me is to be yourself."

"Me being neurotic is that appealing to you?"

I flashed my most charming grin. "What can I say? Quirks really get me going."

"Then that makes you the perfect boyfriend for me."

"I'm pretty sure that means we're a match made in Heaven—and I'm not just saying that since your mom seems to be thriving in her new career as a paranormal matchmaker."

Elias cracked up at my description, which was a relief because I belatedly realized he might not be in a place to joke about her after spending his first birthday without her. "That sounds like something you should write a book about."

"If I do, she's totally getting a shout-out in the acknowledgements." I hugged Elias closer when he nuzzled against me. "Now, using my great powers of the divine, I'm going to guess blue is your favorite color. What's your second favorite color?"

"Your great powers of the divine can only tell you my first favorite color?"

"Yeah, there's a $19.99 a month subscription fee to gain insights on secondary and tertiary color preferences, which is a bit steep for my tastes. It amazes most people I can guess their favoritest favorite color and they leave it at that."

His little giggle was so damn cute. "Fair enough. It's green, then purple. What are your top three?"

"Blue, red, and rainbow."

"Rainbow's not a color—it's seven."

"Technically, sure," I agreed with a shrug. "But when they're all a gradient blending into each other, rainbow is a single awesome color in my book."

Elias tapped his chin as he considered what to ask next. "What do you think of attorneys?"

"Ooh, breaking out the hardball questions already." We both laughed at my joke. "Do you want a grand, sweeping generalization or something more specific?"

"Most people assume we're all ambulance chasers."

I snorted at the absurdity of the stereotype. "Why would a patent attorney ever chase down an ambulance?"

"Exactly! Those stupid personal injury commercials give everyone the worst impression of us. TV shows are even worse, because they convince everyone things happen in a matter of days instead of years with lawsuits."

I could tell that was a mini rant that had been a long time coming. "In general, I guess I assume that most attorneys enjoy arguing and are detail oriented. I don't get the sense that you enjoy the arguing part, though."

"I hate conflict and fighting, but a well-made legal argument can be fun sometimes. Originally, I didn't want to be an attorney, because I didn't want to live at the office like Dad did. But in high school, my best friend's father was also a lawyer, and he was around all the time and always enjoying himself. It made me realize Dad was making a choice to work those kinds of hours, which meant I could choose not to do the same. And it turns out I enjoyed law and was good at it, so I pursued it."

"Did your dad force you into following in his footsteps?"

"No, he tried to talk me out of it when I brought it up," Elias replied. "I took it personally at first, because I made it mean he didn't think I had what was necessary to be an excellent attorney. But he finally admitted it was because he was scared that I might turn into him."

I hugged him tighter. "That's both sweet and sad at the same time."

"Sometimes I suspect the reason he wanted me to work at Rhys's was so he could ensure I was keeping a proper work-life balance. It's ironic since Dad used to be so terrible about that, but he's getting better now. He even left the office early today to prepare dinner for us. That was huge."

"It's often the small things that are the most important."

"You're right."

My next question was more of a practical one. "What are your parents' names? I feel bad calling them just your mom and dad."

"Genevieve and Elijah. I love my mom's name, but I'm glad they named me after Dad. I would have made a terrible Gene."

It was so appropriate for his unusual mother had that kind of name. "Yeah, you're definitely not a Gene, but you could have rocked it as Vieve."

"Maybe as a drag queen."

My dick perked up at the mental image of Elias in full drag, but I stopped that thought before I got carried away and betrayed myself for the pervert I was. Or at least I tried, until I imagined him in black lace panties. *Fuck.* "God, you'd be so sexy as a drag queen."

I didn't expect him to crack up in peals of laughter. "Oh, please. I've never been sexy a day in my life."

"You know, when you say shit like that, it *really*

makes me want to prove you wrong."

It was cute how incredulous he got. "What's sexy about an awkward nerd?"

"Are you trying to test my limits?"

"What do you mean?"

Never one to hold my tongue, I admitted the truth. "My semi will turn into a full hard on unless we change the topic to something benign, like what's your favorite yogurt or shade of beige."

Even the way he looked utterly baffled was cute. "I don't understand."

"The visual of you in drag as Vieve started it, then picturing showing you how sexy you are as a guy made it worse. I'm trying hard to be polite, but you're tempting me something fierce."

He blushed a bright scarlet that went to the tips of his ears. "*Oh*."

"I don't want to make you uncomfortable or pressured, which is why I'm trying to be on my best behavior. The last thing I want is to come on too strong and scare you off."

He was silent for a long moment as he stared at his hands in his lap, rubbing them anxiously as he collected his thoughts.

I cursed myself for fucking up. Why did my dick always have to get in between me and my common sense?

"There's—" He stopped to take a deep breath before continuing. "There's a part of me that wants you to show me how sexy you think I am. But the rest of me has been through a lot of ups and downs today and knows I shouldn't be making that kind of big decision right now."

When he still wouldn't look at me, I tilted his chin so our gazes could meet. "I understand and completely respect that. It's the absolute right call to make. I meant it when I said I wasn't trying to pressure you into anything you don't want."

"But I do want it, eventually," he whispered. "And I don't want to lose you, but right now—"

I gently cut him off. "You don't have to justify or defend your decision to me, Elias. I'm not upset that you're doing the right thing. I'm sorry for making you uncomfortable. All I intended to do was let you know that I absolutely find you sexy, and I'm very much looking forward to showing you that someday. Trust me, I'm already on cloud nine because you want to be my boyfriend and kissed me. I don't need to do everything the first night to be satisfied, okay? I'm happy, and I'm not going anywhere." They were words I never imagined I'd say, but I meant every one of them.

Relief washed over him, making it easier for me to breathe. I never wanted to upset him. "Thank you. My last boyfriend always demanded things that made me uncomfortable and threatened to leave me if I didn't give in and do what he wanted. I guess it did more damage than I realized."

It took effort to bite back a threat at the bastard who would treat him that way. "I'll never get mad or disappointed about you setting boundaries. The only thing that would upset me is if I hurt you because you're too scared to tell me no. I'd much rather suffer from permanent blue balls than do that to you." That comment finally got him to crack a smile. "I'll wait however long you need me to. Please don't feel bad or rush into something you're not comfortable with because you think that's what I need for us to stay together. I'm glad that I'm with you at all, okay?"

"I appreciate that."

To reassure him, I leaned over and pressed a tender kiss to his forehead. "All I ever want is for you to be happy."

He hugged me tightly, allowing me to feel him trembling from his emotions. It made me extra protective of him as I held him close. *Hey, Genevieve. Do us both a favor and go haunt the shit out of his asshole ex-boyfriend Exorcist-style. Get some proper revenge on him for hurting Elias, if you haven't already.*

"I am happy." His contented sigh forced me to tamp down on the lust it sent shooting through me like wildfire, while also mourning his loss when he sat back. "I'm happier today than I ever thought would be possible after losing Mom."

"Good, and we're going to keep it that way. So, what piece of trivia do you know that's very interesting but completely useless?"

"Orgasms cure hiccups."

I blinked at him, convinced I misheard him. "What?"

"Orgasms cure hiccups."

"Okay, now you're just fucking with me. There's no way you said that *orgasms* cure *hiccups*."

He laughed, the last traces of his upset disappearing. "You can look it up. Dr. Francis Fesmire won an Ig Nobel Prize in 2006 for his medical case report on terminating intractable hiccups with digital rectal massages. The most effective method was doing that with a resulting orgasm to cure hiccups."

"Okay, back up. For starters, what's an Ig Nobel Prize?"

"While it's kind of a satire of the Nobel Peace Prize, real Nobel Laureates hand out the prizes. It's an award for unusual achievements in science, medicine, and technology that make you laugh, then think."

Talk about a mind-blowing piece of information. "Are you seriously telling me that orgasms cure hiccups yet somehow it's not common knowledge? And, more importantly, do you have personal experience with this?"

The blush returned to his cheeks. "Yes, and yes. According to who told me, it's successful with regular orgasms, too, not just rectal ones."

It wasn't hard for me to connect the dots after reading his birthday card. Any mom who wrote about giving her son private time to jerk off would probably be open about that kind of thing. "Genevieve told you about this, didn't she?"

He hid his face in his hands with a groan. "Yeah."

"If it makes you feel any better, both my mom and sister would have regaled me about it in graphic detail if they found out about this before me." They were going to laugh their asses off once I told them. "Damn, I have never been so excited to get hiccups in my life. If it works, it's definitely not a useless piece of trivia."

"What's your interesting but useless trivia?"

"It's illegal to die in Longyearbyen, which is an island town in Svalbard, Norway."

His embarrassment was forgotten as he laughed. "That's impossible! You can't make it illegal to die."

"Sure you can. They can't bury people safely in Svalbard because of the permafrost, so if you're about to die, they fly you to mainland Norway to pass away there. Since it's so cold, bodies can't decompose, which means deadly viruses stay alive and put the population at risk. They also banned cats from Svalbard to protect birds. It's a beautiful place, but the four straight months of darkness and freezing cold are too much for me to handle. Plus, no cats are a total deal breaker for me."

"I've never heard of dying being illegal."

"It's not just Norway. There's also a sacred island in Japan called Itsukushima, where no births or deaths are permitted to maintain the sanctity of the land.

There aren't any cemeteries or hospitals, either. It's been that way since, like, the 1800s or something."

Elias snuggled against me once more. "I love random stuff like that."

"Oh, then you'll adore West. She's full of bizarre factoids."

"Can I ask why her name isn't South? North and South are a pair when you think about it."

I couldn't resist running my fingers through his soft hair. "Mom didn't want us to be literal polar opposites of each other. Since East Easton is the actual dumbest name out of that arrangement, she went with West since it's next to North."

"That's actually sweet."

"There's always a logic to Mom's madness. She's convinced that if West had been named South, we wouldn't be as close as we are."

There was a hint of wistfulness in Elias's voice when he said, "It must be nice to have a twin."

"We have our moments. Sometimes she's a real pain in the ass, though. If you think I don't have a filter, wait until you meet her. Not to mention my mom. It's sort of genetic, sorry."

"I'm looking forward to it."

It was too much to hope for that West and Mom wouldn't embarrass me in front of Elias. I'd be in for a lot of good-natured ribbing, but I was still excited to introduce him to my family. They were sure to adore him as I did.

Chapter Seven

ELIAS

NORTH and I stayed up all night talking about everything. His stories were endlessly fascinating, and I enjoyed learning more about him. However, after such a long and emotional day, I was ready to drop by the time the gray dawn started creeping in through my blinds. As I rested my head against the back of my couch, I was losing the battle with sleepiness.

"Hey, it's getting late," he said, sounding reluctant to go.

"Actually, it's getting early now."

I loved his roguish grin. "Still, I should leave and let you get some sleep before dinner tonight."

It was only because I was so tired that I accidentally offered, "Or, you could stay here, and we could go to Callum's together later. You know, if you wanted to."

"I'm cool with crashing on your couch if you are."

I appreciated that he was great about respecting my boundaries. The problem was, that wasn't what I wanted. My exhaustion lowered my guard enough to allow me to be more proactive than normal. "Don't be silly. There's plenty of room in my bed." A thrilling jolt ran through me as he perked up at the prospect. "It's just sleeping."

"I'm totally down for that, thanks."

It took effort to peel myself off the couch. "You can use the bathroom out here to get ready."

"Sounds good."

I headed to the one attached to my bedroom. It gave me time to question if maybe I was making a mistake in offering to let North sleep in my bed. What if I was sending mixed signals, and he thought it was a veiled offer for sex? My inner prude chided me for inviting a man into my bed after only our second meeting. Then again, it wasn't like I was planning on having sex with him—not that there was anything wrong with that if I did. But after I rushed into a relationship with Josh so quickly after losing Mom, I had promised myself I'd be more careful about getting involved with someone. But North's easygoing nature calmed my fears I was making a poor decision. It was too late to change my mind, so I pushed my doubts from my mind.

When I exited my bathroom, he was standing in

front of my dresser, looking at a picture of Mom and me on vacation in Barcelona. We did a monthlong European tour to celebrate me graduating law school, which had been a blast. Most people would have thought I was weird for enjoying hanging out with my mother that much, but every day had been a fun adventure with her.

"No wonder you're so damn cute. Your mom was a total babe."

Despite the sadness that tugged in my heart that I'd never have another vacation like that one with her, I had to laugh at his description. "She definitely would have agreed with your assessment."

He grinned at me as a flutter of nervousness washed over me about getting into bed with him, even if it was only to sleep. "Which side do you want me on?"

I knew it was silly to have a preference, but I had always slept on the right side. When I dated Josh, he had insisted I sleep on the left, and I had been too meek to stand up about something that didn't matter. But every awful morning, I remembered the adage about waking up on the wrong side of the bed. There was a sense of wrongness about it that spoke to much deeper issues between us. "Do you mind the left side?"

"Nope, because that's my favorite one."

"Seriously? You're not just saying that?"

He walked over to his side as I moved to mine. "God's honest truth. Should I sleep in my clothes, or is it okay if I strip down to my boxers?"

My curiosity got the better of me, because I suspected he'd have something other than a plain plaid pattern. "I'm okay with that."

"Awesome." He pulled off his shirt and threw it aside, showing off his toned body that came from an active lifestyle rather than hours at the gym. I blushed as he took off his jeans next, revealing bright rainbow-striped boxers. As I expected, they were as colorful as him. "Should I stay on my side of the bed, or can we cuddle?"

The offer got my hopes up. Neither of my exes had enjoyed cuddling, since they complained I was too clingy for wanting to do that. The few times they had indulged me in the beginning of our relationship had been begrudgingly with much huffing involved. I anxiously tugged on the hem of my shirt as I asked, "You want to?"

"Hell yeah I do, but only if you do, too. I don't want to make you uncomfortable."

I had spent a shameful number of nights wishing someone would hold me after I lost Mom. Even when I had dated Josh, he had always stayed as far from me as the bed would allow. He only touched me when he wanted sex. As soon as he finished, he either got in the shower immediately or rolled over to sleep, regardless if I had come or not. Accepting such horrible treatment was pathetic, but I had been so desperate for a shred of affection I had accepted his meager scraps he tossed out of pity.

The thought of North wanting to hold me without having to beg for it made me almost giddy. I normally slept in a shirt and my briefs, but the promise of skin-to-skin contact after so long was too much temptation to resist. My hand trembled as I removed my glasses and set them on my nightstand. Without being able to see him clearly, it was easier to take off my shirt. Even though he was blurry, I could still feel North's gaze on me like a physical caress. Taking a deep breath to steady myself, I got into bed.

He took it as a cue to do the same. "Do you have a preference?"

"About?"

"Being the big spoon or the little one?"

It was an endearingly childish way to describe cuddling positions. I tried not to be embarrassed as I replied, "I like being held."

He reached over and caressed my cheek with so much tenderness that I got choked up. "You really are perfect."

Rolling onto my side, I faced away from him. "I don't think that qualifies me as being perfect."

"I love being the big spoon, but because I'm only five six, I always end up being the little one. In their defense, it's probably super weird to be a giant and you've got some shorty trying to cuddle you from behind."

His description made me laugh. "I'll take your word for it."

North pressed close to me, tucking his knees behind mine as he pulled me back against his chest. He draped his arm over me, holding me as if I were the most precious thing in the world to him. After going so long without the comfort I craved, I could have cried from how comforting it felt to be embraced by him. It was even better without shirts between us, allowing me to be completely connected with him in that moment. I relaxed further with a contented sigh, surrendering myself to him.

"Damn, this feels amazing." He nuzzled against me, sending a shiver through me. "Almost as if you were made for me to hold."

"Mm-hmm." I didn't trust myself to say anything more than that. Not when being embraced by him had me ready to sign up for a lifetime of cuddles with him, despite barely knowing him. It was everything I had wished for from a boyfriend, and even better than I had dreamed.

"There's not a delicate way to put this, so I'm going to be blunt, okay?"

I didn't know what that meant, but hopefully it was nothing bad. "Sure."

"Please don't get offended or feel obligated to do anything when I wake up with a hard-on later."

Having half expected something terrible, I couldn't stop myself from laughing in relief. "When, and not if?"

"Hey, you're lucky I don't have a boner right now when my dick is this close to your beautiful ass." His words filled me with a flush of heat. "First thing in the morning before my brain is awake, there's no way I'm going to wake up not turned on as fuck by you. I figured I should give you a fair warning."

"Um, thank you?" I wasn't sure what else I could say to that strange compliment.

"I should be the one thanking you for letting me spend tonight with you. Happy birthday, Elias." North pressed a gentle kiss against my shoulder, setting off explosions inside me.

Closing my eyes to savor the moment, I knew I'd replay the memory later when I was alone in bed and wishing I had someone with me. Considering I had expected the day to be a day full of tears and misery, ending it on such a warm and fuzzy note was an unexpected yet welcome surprise. As much as I wanted to linger in consciousness, memorizing every detail of being wrapped up in North's embrace, sleep quickly claimed me.

THE FIRST THING I noticed when I woke up was that North was still embracing me from behind. I then became aware of his hard-on pressing against my ass. That led me to discover that he wasn't the only aroused one. *Oh.*

I had woken up to countless traumatic mornings of Josh trying to have sex with me before I was awake. He had felt entitled to my body, whether or not I was conscious. Too scared to disappoint him, I inevitably gave in to his demands because it hurt more when I resisted. The only saving grace was he was always a fast finisher and would go take a shower alone. How many mornings had I started in tears over the three months we were together? Too many to count.

But North wasn't forcing himself on me. Not only had he given me the courtesy of warning it would happen, but he had given me permission to ignore it. I used to dread whenever Josh got aroused, because unsatisfying rough sex was quick to follow. But North's erection didn't fill me with that same apprehension I used to have with my ex. Instead, I almost had a jittery sense of anticipation coursing through me. Every reflexive brush of his thumb against my skin sent tendrils of lust racing through me, which was why my own hardness was loudly demanding attention.

Rather than acting on it, I gave myself the time to grow accustomed to the thought that he wanted me. Unlike Josh, who had used me as a stepping-stone to convince my father to promote him at work, North had no ulterior motives for wanting to date me. He liked me for me and had accepted things about me I wasn't proud of, like checking my horoscope every morning. I had never met anyone who was so open and carefree, who spoke their mind without second guessing themselves. After Josh lied to me during our entire relationship, North's honesty was something I treasured. I hadn't known him very long, but my trust in him didn't seem misplaced.

He also had a boyish charm that captivated me. Combined with his good looks, it was hard not to get swept away over someone that handsome, outgoing, and fun being interested in a shy, quiet guy like me. But the more we had talked last night, the more I had opened up to him. His warmth drew me in, as did the fact that he genuinely seemed to care about me, despite having just met. There was a powerful pull of attraction between us, and judging by his hardness pressed against me, I wasn't the only one who felt it.

After being hurt by Josh, it would be easy to run away scared. Maybe I was making the same mistake of getting in too deep and too fast into another relationship, but North seemed like a risk worth taking. It was illogical to feel he was Mom-approved after reading my birthday card last night. However, the coincidences were eerie enough to make me wonder if maybe she really was nudging fate to bring him into my life when I needed him most. If anyone could pull that feat off, it'd be her.

I was curious to see his reaction to our current situation. Would he go back on his word and demand I get him off? Or would he sheepishly slink into the bathroom, hoping I hadn't noticed his predicament? As a test, I rocked against his hardness. His soft groan made my cock twitch in the confines of my briefs. I needed to hear him make that sound again, so I repeated my action.

The feel of his fingers trailing against my skin as he moved his hand up to my hip sent electricity jolting through me. His name slipped past my lips as a needy whisper, causing him to freeze against me.

"What do you want me to do?"

"Touch me." My boldness shocked me, but I ached for more. Had I ever been so turned on before?

"Where?"

My need for more made me sound wanton as I dared to demand what I couldn't believe I wanted so much. "Everywhere."

North trailed his hand from where it rested on my hip, down my thigh, then ran it up between my legs. I held my breath when he hesitated before going any higher up my underwear. "Even here?"

"Please."

"Are you sure? I meant it when I said you didn't have to do anything about my—"

I guided him to cup my erection straining in my

briefs so he would understand he wasn't the only one with a bad case of morning wood. "*Please.*"

"Good morning, gorgeous." He rubbed my hardness with a pleased rumble. "Over the underwear only, or can we get rid of them?"

That he asked instead of assuming what I was comfortable with made it easier for me to consent. "Off."

He slid my briefs down, caressing my bare ass in the process. I kicked them the rest of the way off, my heart racing at the promise of what was about to happen.

Rather than touching me, he kept his hand on my hip, brushing against the ridge of my bone with his thumb. "Can I see you?"

I was too aroused to grasp what he meant. "See me?"

"You're not some faceless rando I don't care about as I get you off. I want to kiss you good morning and watch you enjoy yourself."

I was so used to my partner not caring about my pleasure that it hadn't even occurred to me that North might derive enjoyment out of watching my reactions. I rolled over to face him. "Really?"

"Yeah, really. Why does that surprise you?"

Not wanting to fess up to my embarrassing past of being with guys who didn't care about my desires, I replied with a more neutral answer. "My last boyfriend had a strict no kissing before brushing teeth rule."

"That's so stupid." North moved in and gave me a soft kiss that sent my desire into overdrive. "I'd still want to make out with you, even if you just ate a whole plate full of garlic knots."

"And you say you're not a romance author."

"At this rate, you're going to turn me into one." His amusement morphed into hunger. "Why don't you get on top of me so I can make you feel really nice?"

Josh and Will had both refused to let me do that because their masculine egos demanded they always be in charge. As someone who was naturally passive, I had been fine with that mostly. It was only once I was trapped and powerless under Josh's larger form that it had become an issue.

I moved to straddle over North, the sheets falling off me as I situated myself. It wasn't until I was over him that I realized how exposed I was. To my irritation, my nerves and insecurities infringed on my enjoyment. I had always been scrawny with poor self-confidence, despite my mother's best efforts to build me up. When I couldn't make out his facial expression because of my nearsighted vision, my anxiety whispered that he'd be disappointed with what he saw and regret his request. Fears of not being good enough threatened to engulf me as I struggled not to spiral out of control of my emotions. He was young and attractive, so he had surely been with people much hotter and less damaged than me. Why would he ever settle for me when he could have anyone he wanted?

North sat up and cupped my face between his hands, his eyebrows furrowed with concern. "What's wrong?"

That close, I could see the genuine worry in his expression. It tugged at my heart, making me feel even more terrible for assuming he'd think the worst of me. "I'm sorry."

"Sorry for what?" He brushed his thumbs against my cheekbones. "Tell me what's going through your head right now. Help me understand."

I had to look up at my ceiling as I struggled. Apparently being treated with kindness was more than I could handle. Why was I so broken? "Sorry I'm such a mess."

Neither Josh nor Will had patience for my emotions. I braced myself for North to become disgusted with me and storm out of my apartment like they would have. Instead, he hugged me, stroking my hair to soothe away my worries. "You have nothing to be sorry for, Elias. I told you before, we don't have to do anything you don't want to."

"But I want to," I whispered. My erection that had yet to wane was still standing as a testament to that fact. "When I'm like this—"

He pulled back to look at me in confusion. "Like what?"

"I'm overly emotional, and damaged, and gawky, and—"

"Wait, are you worried I'm not attracted to you?"

I nodded miserably.

"How many times do I have to tell you that you're perfect before you believe me? I'm not saying that to get in your pants, Elias. I genuinely believe it, which my hard-on should definitely prove to you." It shifted under me, which only intensified my arousal, despite my current state of upset. "We can talk this out if you want, or I can show you how wrong your asshole ex-boyfriends are for making you feel this way."

I was scared to be brave, but I persisted despite my insecurities. "Show me."

When North kissed me this time, it wasn't a gentle good-morning greeting. He claimed my lips, his tongue delving into my mouth to tease me into a frenzy. His hands caressed me all over, helping me forget my hang-ups. I was so caught up in his passion, that I didn't notice he had guided me into a position where I was pinning him against the bed.

Acting on instinct, I rocked my hardness against his as he kissed me into oblivion. It was amazing, so I moved my hips with more urgency as I frotted against him. A burning need for more replaced all my worries. However, my last brain cell reminded me I was being as bad as my exes had been. "Wait, wait, wait."

Unlike them, he stopped what he was doing and didn't get angry with me for it. "What?"

"This isn't fair to you."

North laughed but not unkindly. "Do I sound like I have any complaints?"

"But I'm being horribly selfish only chasing after my own pleasure."

"One, I was getting as much satisfaction as you, so no you weren't. Two, if you're comfortable with me taking off my underwear, I'm down to jerk each other off while we make out if that'll help you feel less selfish—which again, I don't think you were being. We can also keep doing what we were doing or stop if you need to."

That he was willing to quit if that was what I wanted made it an easier decision. "Is it really fine if we take care of each other?"

"More than fine."

I moved so North could shimmy out of his underwear, freeing his hardness. Being able to see it without my glasses made my eyes widen in surprise. It was yet another impressive way he differed from my exes.

He repositioned us so we were both leaning back against propped up pillows. "Do you want to touch me first to get comfortable?"

How did he always seem to know what I needed? "Is that okay?"

"Of course. Just tell me when it's my turn to start."

There was a slight tremble in my hand as I reached down to touch temptation. My cheeks were pink with embarrassment as I ran my fingertips along the rigid length, marveling at how long it was. As I wrapped my fingers around his impressive girth, I was equal parts excited and fearful about what that would mean for my ass later. I cautiously worked his hardness, the familiar action feeling strange when doing it on someone else.

North leaned over for a teasing kiss, running one of his free hands down my chest to toy with my nipple. His searing kisses and light touch stirred my desire, but he never moved below the waist as he waited for my consent.

When he moaned against my lips, it filled me with enough confidence to tell him, "Your turn."

To my surprise, he didn't instantly go for the prize. Instead, he continued kissing me as his hand drifted further south. His meandering path built up my arousal until it was almost maddening. It was a relief when he finally took my aching arousal in hand.

While I had been timid with my touch, North jerked me off with a tight grip that I thrust into. I mimicked him by adjusting my hold, earning me a breathy "So good" as I picked up the pace.

I soon lost myself in the dizzying blur of giving and receiving pleasure. His ardent kisses sent me high into the stratosphere of arousal as we jacked each other off at the same time. I never imagined something so simple could be so mind-blowingly incredible.

As I neared my end, it became increasingly difficult to stay on rhythm of stroking North. My muscles tightened in anticipation as the feeling built up inside me, until it snapped in a chaotic burst of ecstasy. I came with a soft cry, thrusting into North's fist until I finished.

My mind blanked of anything other than the intense satisfaction thrumming through me, but my body's autopilot mercifully kicked on and allowed me to finish North off. He moaned my name as he climaxed, giving me a tender kiss when he was done.

We both sat still for a few moments as we returned to ourselves. My earlier anxiety seemed so foolish in the face of feeling so incredible. Even though we had only touched each other to get off, it was the single most satisfying sexual experience I had ever had. It also caused me to realize something surprising. "*Wow.*"

"I'd say," North agreed with a playful arrogance. "Why do you seem shocked?"

"Because that was a first for me. A few firsts, actually."

"What do you mean?"

"I've never done that for a guy before."

North's eyebrows arched upward in shock. "Seriously?"

"Will and Josh both said if they wanted jerked off, they'd do it themselves."

He shook his head. "Damn, that's some fucked up backward thinking. Yeah, jacking off by yourself is one thing, but it's different when you're doing it to pleasure someone else."

"They didn't really care about that."

"What, you mean about pleasuring you?"

In my euphoric state, I lacked the ability to hold back my thoughts from the person responsible for me feeling so good. "That's why I've never finished first until now."

North seemed baffled by my response. "Wait, are you saying this was your first time coming first *ever*?"

"Yeah," I sheepishly admitted. "Once they got off, I was on my own. Will said it wasn't his fault it took me so long to come, and Josh always slept or showered by himself when he finished."

He looked horrified before anger came over him. "What giant fucking assholes!" When I winced from him raising his voice in his outrage, he apologized. "Shit, I'm sorry. That's just so fucked up. I'm upset on your behalf, because that is some serious bullshit."

I shrugged, because I didn't have a defense against something that was true. "It's my fault for being stupid, but—"

"No, don't blame yourself because they're selfish bastards. This is one hundred percent on them for being fucking shit weasels."

"But I was foolish for being with them. I dated Will when I first went to college, because I was homesick and ashamed over never having been with someone before. Josh approached me after Mom's funeral, and I was so lost in my grief, I wasn't thinking straight and—"

He gently cut me off once more. "Hey, look at me." When I was too humiliated to, he guided my chin up with his clean hand. "Listen. They were both enormous assholes for taking advantage of you. What they did wasn't okay, and you didn't deserve that. They may have convinced you it was your fault, but that's all on them."

I needed off the emotional roller coaster I was on as tears once again welled up inside me despite how incredible I physically felt. It was embarrassing to confess the shameful truth of the situation. "All I wanted was for someone to love me and not be alone anymore. But I ended up hurt and more alone than before."

After two ex-boyfriends who hated when I became upset, I expected North to leave in disgust. Instead, he pulled me into a crushing hug, uncaring of the mess between us. "You're not alone now. I promise I'll do my best to take care of you, and I don't just mean sexually. I want to be there for you and always make sure you know that you're loved."

I clung to him and tried to resist being swept away from my tumultuous reactions. It was almost too much to process that he sounded like he really meant it.

He didn't push me off him or tell me to get over myself. Instead, he held me as he gave me the space to sort through my emotions in peace, rubbing my back in silent comfort. I soaked it in, letting him heal my old wounds from a time in my life I wished I could forget. In some respects, that was even better than the sexual gratification I had experienced with him.

I wasn't sure how long we stayed like that, but I never wanted to leave the only sanctuary I had found since losing Mom.

AFTER FINISHING BREAKFAST, I still suffered from lingering embarrassment over my behavior in bed. Even though North had been patient with me, I felt bad that my anxiety had almost ruined our time together. Nervously twisting my glass of water on the kitchen table, I steeled my nerves to say what I needed to. "I owe you an apology about earlier."

"Why?"

His puzzled reaction threw me. "I probably made you uncomfortable when I got emotional, but—"

"You don't have to apologize for that. If anything, I'm sorry I overwhelmed you."

"No, that was all my own anxiety. I appreciate you being so patient with me as I worked through it."

He gave me a sympathetic look. "It sounds like your exes really did a number on you."

"I'm starting to realize that." While I knew I had leftover issues from my two broken relationships, I hadn't realized how much damaging emotional baggage I was still carrying from them. "I shouldn't have let them get in my head and ruin everything."

North reached over and gave my hand a reassuring squeeze. "They didn't ruin anything. As long as you enjoyed yourself, so did I."

"I did, but I feel bad for assuming you'd react the same way they did. That's unfair to you when you're nothing like them."

"Look at it like this. Sometimes it takes a while to detox from unhealthy things, right? When you're used to situations turning out for the worst, of course you'll expect that to happen. What matters is that you pushed through it and enjoyed yourself despite your past trying to hold you back. It takes time to deprogram, you know? You should be more patient with yourself."

They were wise words from someone so young, but my heart still feared rejection. "That doesn't scare you?"

"Why would I be scared of getting to be the good example that proves why those assholes weren't worthy of you?" His self-assured grin was so charming, I couldn't help but smile back. "I'm not going to get mad at you for wincing in anticipation of something painful happening when they trained you to expect that. You haven't known me long enough to trust that I won't turn around and do the same thing to you they did. Because I'm sure they were both decent guys in the beginning and didn't reveal their true nature until you were too deep to break free easily."

It was such a relief hearing someone acknowledged my exes had baited-and-switched me. "That's exactly what happened."

"It happens to a lot of people, me included."

That surprised me, because he didn't seem like the kind of guy who was gullible enough to be misled. "Really?"

"Oh, yeah. I've had more than one encounter with a dude who seemed super chill at the bar, then after we got back to his place, he'd turn into a psycho. Abusive assholes are great at hiding their true nature for as long as it takes to get what they want."

"But you're brave enough to walk out on them. I stayed because I was a coward."

"You'd think that, but I've absolutely done things I'm not proud of because I was too scared of what the guy would do to me if I said 'no.' It was easier to get it over with and sneak out once he fell asleep than risk what would happen in a confrontation if I refused to do what he wanted. That doesn't make you a coward; it makes you smart. You can't beat yourself up for doing what you had to for the sake of self-preservation."

I stared at North in shock, almost unable to wrap my mind around the fact that someone as confident as him had been in the same predicament as me. "But didn't that make you hate yourself?"

"Why should I hate myself when they're the asshole?" He shrugged like it was no big deal. "It's not like I was going, 'Oh, I hope this guy is abusive and treats me like shit tonight.' It was always a case of they were hot, charming, and saying all the right things to lure me into their trap. I'm a pretty good judge of character, but when they're masters of being manipulative dicks, they fool the best of us. We aren't the ones in the wrong, so I refuse to feel badly about it."

"You can choose not to feel bad about it?" It almost sounded like a fictional superpower to me.

"At first, I'd beat myself up for getting taken advantage of and letting myself get put into those situations. I'd berate myself over being stupid enough to let that happen without putting up a fight. But I realized that kind of thinking gave them too much power over me. It pissed me off that it was one more way they were manipulating me when they weren't even there."

It was weird hearing him have the same thought pattern as me with my ex-boyfriends. I listened with rapt attention as he continued.

"I had to give myself permission to place the blame where it belonged—on them for being the ones who did that to me. If I would treat someone else in that situation with compassion and not victim-blame them, why wouldn't I do that for myself? Once I realized that, I could leave that shit in the past where it belongs."

It was like North had opened my eyes. I had spent so much time blaming myself for being weak and getting myself into two abusive relationships that I never held Will and Josh accountable for their toxic actions. If Callum had been in my situation, I wouldn't have blamed him for being too nice and letting people take advantage of him. I would have been angry with the guys for using his kindness against him and hurting him when he didn't deserve it. So why was I so quick to fault my own failings rather than Will and Josh's? Why couldn't I extend that same compassion I would show my friend to myself? "Wow, you're right."

"That's why I didn't get upset with you earlier. That 'screw them' mentality doesn't happen overnight. You have to actively remind yourself when things trigger that thought pattern of why you don't need to feel the way they've trained you to react. Try being kinder to yourself. Those bastards don't deserve to hurt you any more than they already have."

His advice emboldened me to straddle myself over his lap. I hugged him, overcome by a rush of emotions for him. My heart was light and free for the first time in forever, no longer burdened by being forced to bear the full blame for what had happened to me. "Thank you."

The two words were an inadequate expression of the level of my gratitude, especially as he held me. I soaked up the comfort of his strength and assurance to shore up my shaking foundations. My mom had been a firm believer that people came into our lives for a reason. North continued to prove over and over again how much I needed him in mine right now.

Chapter Eight

NORTH

BEFORE I MET CALLUM, Felix had warned me that he was off-limits. He said the poor kid had been through hell and back, and the last thing he needed was for a horny bastard like me to break his heart. Of course, being told I couldn't have him made me want Callum, especially once I saw how damn cute he was.

But Felix had been right. Callum was a pure soul of sunshine, rainbows, and unicorns. He needed to be protected at any cost, which meant my dick was very much staying in my pants. Our whole friend group had banded around him like a bunch of older brothers as we helped him get comfortable after his sudden move to America. That didn't mean I wouldn't enjoy making him blush by embarrassing him from time to time, but he was strictly hands-off for all of us.

We had all been concerned when Callum developed feelings for his new friend, Rune. Whatever we had imagined the man to be, it certainly hadn't been Rune Tourneau, one of the most beautiful people alive. That had been a hell of a surprise over dinner the night Callum introduced him.

The biggest shock of all had been what a cool, down-to-earth guy Rune was. He had a dry sense of humor and was the best cook in the world, which hardly seemed fair. Every time we were lucky enough to go over to Callum's apartment for movie night, Rune would make us the most incredible desserts. It made him even sexier to me than his infamous cologne commercial where he fucked a woman in an elevator, which was saying something.

If Rune had been a normal hot guy dating Callum, it would have been super fucked-up how much I had gotten off to fantasies about him. But the guy in my spank bank was Rune the Model, not Rune the Boyfriend. Besides, it wasn't like I didn't include Callum in our threesomes in my head. I may not be allowed to touch him, but the private theatre in my mind was a different story.

Because of that, every time I visited Callum's apartment, I had a permanent semi the whole visit. Rune exuded sex pheromones and smelled like lust, so it wasn't my fault. It was a given that I would have to jerk off as soon as I got home after hanging out with them.

But for the first time, I had spent an entire evening

alone with Callum and Rune without being horny as hell for either of them. Elias consumed my every thought. I wanted him more than I had ever wanted anyone else. But I wasn't interested in a hit-it-and-quit-it fling. I longed to help heal the damage his abusive exes had inflicted, make him laugh, and forget what pain was. My goal was to learn every single thing about him that made him tick and hear more stories about his awesome mom. I couldn't wait to introduce him to my family so they could love him as much as I already did. It shouldn't have been surprising I had fallen for him so hard and fast, given that nobody in my family did anything normal. However, it still amazed me I was so serious about him when I was rarely serious about anything.

I hadn't expected it to be so heartwarming seeing Callum and Elias interacting. Everyone in our friend group was super outgoing and extroverted, which had drawn Callum out of his shell the longer he had hung out with us. But Callum and Elias were both shy introverts who opened up to each other because of how comfortable they were with one another as kindred spirits. Rune also seemed far more at ease with the quieter evening. The three of them were in perfect harmony with each other and all on the same wavelength. I was definitely the dumbest guy in a room full of geniuses. Good thing hearing Elias talk smart was sexy as fuck or I'd have a complex.

After a delicious dinner of honey garlic glazed

salmon, Elias was aglow with happiness. It was so cute that I wondered if I could convince Rune to teach me how to cook. I could make pasta, but anything beyond that was probably going to end in a culinary disaster.

"Thanks for such an incredible night. I'm not used to people making a fuss over my birthday, so I really appreciate it."

"I'm glad you enjoyed it," Rune said with a kind smile that would have sold a million magazines if he had been photographed for the front cover.

In true Callum fashion, he insisted, "Wait until you try dessert." His sweet tooth was unrivaled. Rune must give him one hell of a nightly workout to burn off that many calories to keep his boyfriend so slender. Callum brightened when there was a knock on the front door. "Great, your surprise is here!"

"My surprise?"

I couldn't resist joking about it. "Please tell me that's a stripper."

Rune made an amused noise at my words as he went to answer the door. He had barely opened it all the way before getting enveloped in a crushing hug that drove him back a few steps. Wearing a teal button-down with a purple T-shirt under it and jeans, the man was blond, blue-eyed, and so drop-dead gorgeous that he would have made me think perverse thoughts if my brain wasn't so full of Elias.

A second man entered the apartment with a bemused expression, carrying two wrapped presents.

Equally handsome, with delicate features, high cheekbones, and the sexiest eyebrows I had ever seen, he looked imminently fuckable in his black suit and green shirt that brought out the color in his eyes. Everything about the man was elegant perfection. "You're hugging him like you haven't seen him in three years and not three days."

The man clinging to Rune like a determined octopus hugged him even tighter with a sexy smirk. "Aww, is my pookie jealous?" His question earned him a long-suffering eye roll.

"Don't you have other people to hug?" Rune asked as he tried to detangle himself from the man's grasps.

"Fine, I'll go shower someone else with love." He turned his sights on Callum, who got up to greet him. Like Rune, he gathered Callum in a fierce hug. I didn't know who he was, but Callum made a happy noise as he accepted the show of affection.

"Xander, Jules, what are you doing here?" Elias asked in amazement.

"It's not a birthday without a proper birthday hug." The hugger held his arms open to Elias next. I felt a flare of jealousy when he got up to accept the man's embrace. "It's great to see you again, Elias."

"You, too. Have you been well?"

"Always," the man replied with a charming grin. "So, who's the cutie with you?"

I arched an eyebrow at the label; it wasn't one

typically applied to me, especially when I was in the same room as Callum. "Hi, I'm North. Nice to meet you."

When I held my hand out to shake his, he pulled me into a hug. It was a proper one and not a wimpy loose arm around the shoulders air embrace. "Likewise. I'm Jules, and the scowly one is my boyfriend, Xander."

Rune and Xander came over to take their seats at the table, but not before Jules gave a hug to his boyfriend so he wouldn't feel left out. It was adorable how it made Xander smile as he lingered in their embrace for a moment longer than was necessary. "Jules is my older brother and a notorious hugger. Sorry."

No wonder the guy was so sexy. "It's cool."

"Xander is also my boss," Callum added. That clarified who the men were, but not why they were there or why Elias seemed delighted by their presence as they joined us at the table.

"I asked Callum if we could come over tonight to give Elias his birthday present in person, since doing it at work is no fun," Jules explained.

A slight blush graced Elias's cheeks. "Oh, you didn't have to get me anything!"

"We wanted to," Xander assured him as he passed over a flat box covered in metallic silver paper with gold trimming. "This one is from me."

"The tasteful monochrome gave that away," Jules

teased. I glanced at the other present, which was a medium-size box with rainbow glitter wrapping paper. Although they were strangers to me, there was no mistaking who was giving which gift.

Xander rolled his eyes but said nothing as Elias opened it.

After opening the clamshell black leather box, Elias pulled out a blue marble rollerball pen with a subtle twist accented by several narrow silver bars running the length of it. I didn't know they made pens that fancy. He was clearly bowled over by the present. "This is beautiful, but it's too much!"

"Someone with handwriting as lovely as yours deserves a pen worthy of it."

He looked at Xander with awed appreciation. "Thank you, Xander. That's so kind and generous of you. I love it."

"You're most welcome. Happy birthday, Elias."

"Now it's my turn to show off," Jules said as he gestured for Xander to pass his present over to Elias next.

It was precious how Elias was so careful while unwrapping his gift so as not to tear any of it. West and I had always been "shred the wrapping as fast as we could to get to the present quicker" types.

Elias took off the box lid and removed a black wood picture frame with white matting. It was an adorable autographed drawing of a blue kiwi bird that I recognized as being one of the side characters from the popular *Pookie & Bunbun in Love* webcomic. I should have known that he would be a fan of the cute art style that told the love story of a bunny and a unicorn cat. He gasped with delight, "Oh, it's Avery! Thanks, Jules! I adore him!"

As Elias showed the picture to everyone at the table, I said, "That's super precious. He reminds me of your Avery."

"That's because this Avery is the same as the one my mom made for me."

"Elias is too cute not to be a part of my comic, so he kindly let me use his Avery as an avatar for his adventures."

If I thought that was surprising, it was nothing compared to Callum adding, "We're all in it. I'm Cally the hamster, Rune is Pebbles the hedgehog, Jules is Bunbun, and Xander is Pookie."

For someone used to weird shit happening, sitting at a table surrounded by people who were all part of a famous webcomic was high up there on my list of what the fucks. Especially since someone as elegant and poised as Xander being turned into a cute cartoon unicorn cat was mind-boggling. "That's so awesome!"

Jealousy once again burned in me as Elias got up to hug Jules, even as I found it interesting that he didn't go over to Xander. It looked like Jules was the only one with the fortitude to do that to his boyfriend and live to tell the tale.

"Thanks to both of you—to all of you—for making this such a wonderful birthday. It means more to me than I can express. After everything you've done to help me this year, from the bottom of my heart, thank you so much."

I hated being left out of things, and his impassioned gratitude made me wonder what Elias had been alluding to. That was a conversation that would have to wait until we were alone later.

Jules nudged his brother. "Please tell me you're going to make this a proper birthday with a cake."

"Who do you think you're talking to?" Rune asked with an indignant look. "If you behave yourself, maybe I'll let you have a piece of my spiced caramel apple drip cake with candied walnuts."

"That sounds amazing, Rune. Wow." Elias looked overwhelmed by the amount of love that was being shown for him, which was sweet but also a little heartbreaking. I reached over and squeezed his hand under the table. The smile he gave me was radiant and made me fall even deeper in love with him. I'd do damn near anything to keep him smiling always.

AS WE DROVE HOME after a fun night, I finally had the chance to ask Elias the question that had been plaguing me since the unexpected guests had arrived. "How do you know Jules and Xander?"

"I already knew Xander from work because he's Rhys's personal assistant. But how we became friends is sort of a humiliating story."

Although I was burning with curiosity, I told him, "If you don't want to tell me, that's fine. I didn't mean to pry."

"No, it's okay." He took a deep breath as he prepared to fill me in on the secret. "When I got together with Josh back in January after Mom's funeral, I didn't realize he was living with Xander as his long-term boyfriend. Like everyone else in the office, I had assumed that Xander was dating Jules. Plus, Josh assured me that they had broken up a while ago, so I had no reason not to believe him."

That wasn't the type of story I had been expecting to hear. "Meaning Josh was cheating on Xander to be with you?"

"Yeah. I was so naïve; I had no clue." Remorse was written all over Elias's face. "Xander found out about Josh's relationship with me in March and kicked him out of his apartment. Josh moved in with me because I was a fool who bought all of his lies hook, line, and sinker."

I reached over and caressed the back of his neck in comfort. "You didn't know."

"I didn't want to, plus I was so lost in my grief, I didn't care. Everything hurt and was awful, so it seemed like what I deserved."

"No one deserves that, least of all you."

He smiled wanly. "That's exactly what Xander told me. Although he had every reason in the world to hate me, he tried to help me by opening my eyes to what a terrible boyfriend Josh was."

"Wow, that says a lot, doesn't it?" That bastard must have truly been awful to have the person burned by cheating try to save the guy their ex had been with behind their back. It spoke to what kind of man Xander was. My respect for him went up a few notches.

"Deep down, I knew he was right. I was depressed because there wasn't a single positive thing about being with Josh other than I wasn't alone. Being by myself and sad was better than being stuck with him and miserable. But I didn't know how to get myself out of the relationship. I tried to break up with him before the wedding, and he refused."

I had to bite back an incredulous laugh. "What do you mean he refused?"

"When I said we should go our separate ways, he told me to stop being stupid. He claimed I was trying to use my grief to hurt myself by cutting him out of my life. He refused to let me break up with him. Let's leave it at he gave me a punishing reminder that I belonged to him and should never think about leaving him again."

Rage boiled inside of me at the thought of that asshole gaslighting and hurting Elias. If I ever met the son of a bitch, I'd make him regret it for the rest of his days. I was careful to not let my anger bleed into my voice as I kept it gentle. "I'm so sorry, Elias. That sounds like hell."

"That wasn't even the worst of it. We all went to Rhys's second wedding, and Josh was determined to use me to get back at Xander. It was so blindingly obvious that he never cared about me at all. He was just using me like Xander had warned me. I attempted to leave, but he caught me and he—"

When Elias's voice cracked in grief, I stroked the nape of his neck. "You don't have to tell me if it's too much."

"No, I'm okay." After a few calming breaths to steady himself, he continued his story as he drove us back to his apartment. "He dragged me into a supply closet and tried to force himself on me, because he was convinced that Xander would come find us. Josh was obsessed with getting payback on him and Jules. I —I tried to fight him off, but he was so much bigger than me that I couldn't. If Jules hadn't stopped him, I…"

It took a monumental effort to swallow down every angry threat so I didn't add to Elias's trauma. "The important thing is that Jules helped you."

"Now that I know what a light-hearted, fun guy Jules is, the badass who intimidated Josh into leaving is even more unbelievable to me. But realizing that a total stranger who should hate me would stand up for me because of how badly Josh was treating me gave me the strength to break up with him. I don't know how I ever would have done it if the two of us were alone. But with Jules there, Josh couldn't use any of his normal tactics to make me change my mind. I told him to take everything out of my apartment, that I never wanted to see him again. And he left, just like that. It was such an anticlimactic end to the worst time of my life that it made it that much harder to believe it was finally over. All of his things were really gone when I got home."

"I'm so glad you took a stand against that bastard. He can go rot in the deepest circle of Hell, and it still wouldn't be enough."

Elias tightened his grip on the steering wheel before relaxing his hands. "I was so terrified that Josh was going to come back and make me regret doing that. But Jules gave me a hug and told me it was okay, that I was safe now. I broke down sobbing about what had happened, the three months of torture with Josh, losing Mom, all of it came out. It was so humiliating, but every time I apologized, Jules said it was fine, that the only person who should be sorry wasn't there anymore. I was finally safe."

It made me feel like an asshole for getting jealous of Jules earlier. "I'm glad he was there to help you."

"Once I regained my composure, Xander opened the door and saw us hugging in the closet. Because of what Josh had done to me, I was half-undressed, so it looked like we were messing around. I had convinced myself that he blamed me for stealing his boyfriend, so I panicked that he was going to think I was trying to make a move on Jules. But Xander calmed me down and told me he wanted to thank me for helping him get out of his toxic relationship with Josh. I couldn't understand how he didn't blame me at all. They were both so kind to me when they both should have hated me."

"They seem like great guys, so I'm not surprised that they could see that you weren't at fault in that situation."

The tension finally left Elias. "They really are. Once I had calmed down, they invited me to join them at their table with Callum and Rune. Callum had talked to me outside the church, begging me to leave Josh, because he said that wasn't love, that was abuse. He went out of his way to be a close friend, which I hadn't had in such a long time. Xander also looked out for me at work, and Jules started visiting me every time he came to visit him."

"Callum's such a sweetheart. You couldn't ask for a better friend than him."

Elias glanced over at me with a smile. "True. It's amazing how only a few months ago, I was miserable and alone, yet now I have four wonderful friends and an incredible boyfriend who care about me. I'll never stop being grateful to all of you for being there for me in my darkest time."

"You deserve nothing but happiness, Elias. I'll do everything in my power to make you happy."

We stopped at a red light, so he leaned over and gave me a sweet kiss. "Thank you. Truly."

As we continued driving, he told me about his tradition of writing thank-you cards with his mom and how he had written one for Xander and Jules. That explained why he had been gifted such a beautiful pen. He then explained how he became part of Jules's popular webcomic.

Once we parked at his apartment and got out of the car, I gathered him into a tight hug. He had been through so much, and I wanted to wrap him up in a warm blanket and keep him safe from all harm. I didn't want him to suffer again, especially if I could do something about it.

Still not ready for our time to be over, I played the part of the gentleman by walking him to his door. Of course, my secret hope was that he wished I'd stay with him as much as I hoped to be with him. I held my breath as he fished out his keys.

He kept his focus on his task, a slight tremble in his hand as he inserted his key. "I know you probably have other things to do, but if you want to stay a little longer—"

In my eagerness, I couldn't wait for him to finish his invitation. "There's nothing I'd rather do than spend more time with you."

It was cute how Elias bit his lower lip to stop himself from grinning in joy. "Really?"

"Really." I followed him into his apartment, having a momentary debate with myself over how far I should push things. Ever since getting a taste of him earlier that morning, I desperately needed more. I waited until he tossed his keys in a mosaic bowl I assumed his mom had made for him before pulling him into a loose embrace. "In fact, I'd love to keep you up all night as I show you what real pleasure is." It was more important to me after hearing his story in the car.

I took it as a good sign that despite his blush, he didn't pull away from me. The nervous flutter of his eyelashes was extra adorable. "W-what do you want to do?"

"I'm dying to suck your dick."

He stiffened in my arms, his gray eyes wide with shock. "*Why?*"

"I want you, I love giving head, and it sounds like you've never had a boyfriend who wanted you to enjoy yourself to the fullest with oral."

Elias glanced away in shame. "Josh said that was my job."

Rage rippled through me. "Your *job?*"

"Yeah, he had a lot of hang-ups about authority, positions, and masculinity. He refused to get on his knees for anyone, least of all me."

It took significant effort to restrain myself to

swearing, "That selfish fucking bastard!" I calmed myself when my outburst made Elias wince. His reflexive action told me things about his previous relationships that I *really* didn't like. "Sorry, I didn't mean to be loud again. It just pisses me off that he acts like pleasuring you was an arduous chore that he couldn't be bothered with."

"I didn't feel like I was missing out on that much." He shrugged as if that wasn't an enormous fucking problem.

My jaw dropped at his unfathomable claim. "What—how could you—what?"

"Um, well, the thing is, none of it felt good. I thought Will was bad at it, but after Josh, I figured something was wrong with me for not enjoying sex with either of them." He shifted uncomfortably in my hold, unable to look at me. "I wasn't interested in more, because it'd be more of the same, so…"

Pulling him closer in a bear hug, my heart broke for him. It made me ill that he had spent god knows how many years thinking he was the issue, when it was so obvious that both of his exes were selfish assholes only out for themselves. "I'm so sorry they hurt you. I promise it's not always like that."

Elias stepped out of my hold with a frustrated expression. "You say that, but I was obviously the one with the problem for not enjoying being with them."

"I can guarantee that you're not. Trust me, I'll

make you feel so good that you won't ever doubt yourself again."

"That's a bold claim."

"It's a fact. All you need to do is lie there and *feel*. Let me take care of the rest." The promise of getting to do that for him had me rock-hard.

He frowned. "But if I do that, I'm no better than them, because you get nothing out of it."

"See, that's where you're wrong. Pleasuring you *is* pleasurable for me. Making you feel good makes *me* feel good. Hell, the *thought* of making you feel good turns me on." When he looked as if he still didn't believe me, I took his hand and cupped it around my hard-on he had inspired. He stared at me in disbelief but didn't move away. "Does this help you understand how serious I am?"

He rubbed me through my pants, testing my willpower. "How are you this aroused by the thought of making me feel good?"

"Because thinking about kissing you all over, sucking your beautiful dick, and making you moan with ecstasy until you come in my mouth is damn near enough to get me off." I rocked against his palm, feeling like I would go out of my mind if I didn't get some relief soon. "Let me make us both feel better."

I could see the war within him raging on, but he squared his shoulders as he gazed at me with determination. "I'm willing to try."

Rejoicing as he led me to his bedroom, I teased

him with soft kisses as I let my hands wander under his shirt. He shivered as he held on to me for support.

By the time I got both of us naked, he was fully erect. I guided him to make himself comfortable in the center of the bed, then set about covering him with a flurry of kisses and featherlight touches all over. The lower I drifted, the more he squirmed under me. I took my time as I made sure that he lost himself in his feelings instead of overthinking. When he whispered, "Please," I knew I was making progress.

He tensed under me as I trailed my fingertips along his rigid length that I couldn't wait to get in my mouth. But I didn't want to jump straight into it. I wanted to build up the anticipation, so I shifted down to trail kisses up his inner thigh while caressing his other with my hand. My next target was focusing on his balls. Running my tongue down the seam, I sucked on one of them to tease him further. It earned me an interesting noise of surprise.

"That shouldn't feel so good," he said in a shaky voice, looking down at me with confusion.

I stopped what I was doing, placing a lingering kiss before answering him. "You've been lied to. This is just the warm-up."

His response disappeared in a gasp as I switched my attention to the other side, rubbing my lips against it before tonguing it. I then sucked it while stroking his shaft at the same time to drive him wild.

Elias muffled a startled cry behind his hand.

I wouldn't be satisfied until he was overwhelmed with pleasure. "Let me hear you." I licked my way up his balls to the underside of his erection. It earned me a whimper as I neared the tip. "Please, Elias."

When I sucked on the frenulum, he lost his battle to stay silent. "*Oh!*"

"That's it." The head of his cock rested on my lips as I teased it with my tongue, swirling it around the crown. He jerked under me as I toyed with him, drawing in only the first two inches to suck on, before backing off. I licked along his length, then kissed my way back up the underside, making sure each one lingered with a hint of suction. "Just let go and *feel.*"

Satisfied he had the right idea, I went down on him again, taking more of him into my mouth. I held him steady with one hand, while using the other to tease his balls. That earned me another needy keen, which was music to my ears. It got harder for him to smother his sounds of enjoyment as I continued, which was exactly what I wanted. Part of me was dying to blow his mind by teasing his hole at the same time, but I'd save that treat for later.

When I thought he was getting lulled into complacency, it was time to show off a bit. Without warning, I deep-throated him until my nose touched his pubes. He cried out my name, and I moaned around him as I sucked him off.

His fingers entwined in my hair, but he didn't use his grip to force me down. He held on for dear life as I bobbed my head along his entire length. I enjoyed taking him deep, pulling out almost to the tip, then let him go all the way to the back of my throat with a swallow. His glasses fogged up, but he kept them on so he could keep watching me in awe. I put on a hell of a show to ensure he experienced more pleasure in that moment than he had in all his previous times with his shithead exes combined.

Elias's noises reached a fevered pitch as I savored every second of sucking his dick. He had given himself over to his feelings, tossing his head back as his thighs squeezed me hard as he tensed up. His fractured sounds of enjoyment and knowing he was experiencing genuine pleasure for the first time sent me soaring. I had always loved giving blow jobs, but never as much as I did in that moment.

I took him as deep as I could and hummed around him. He arched up from the force of coming hard with a cry. Two quick tugs on my cock and the taste of him were all I needed to finish with a satisfied moan.

Sitting back, I watched him adrift in his intense afterglow. That was almost as enjoyable as what we had just done. There was no way he would ever doubt he was the problem after that. I was proud of how long it took before his brain kicked in and tried to ruin it. "Wait, what about you?"

I held up my cum-covered hand with a grin. "Does this answer your question?"

He spluttered in shock, taking quite a few tries before asking, "You *came*?"

"I told you: making you feel good makes me feel good."

"How could it make you feel *that* good?"

"I meant it when I said that pleasuring you gives me *immense* satisfaction." As I licked off some cum, I wasn't disappointed by his strangled reaction of confused enjoyment. The mix of us on my tongue was the best thing in the world.

He furrowed his eyebrows in confusion. "I don't understand."

I grabbed a tissue off his nightstand to wipe off my hand. "It's simple. If you feel good, I feel good. If you're turned on, I'm turned on. If you come because I made you feel better than anyone ever has before, then hell yeah, I'm going to come, too. Watching you lose yourself in ecstasy is sexy as fuck."

"Even though we didn't have sex?"

I stretched out next to him, gratification thrumming through my body. "Sex is more than getting a dick shoved inside you. You can be intimate without penetration." When he still looked confused, I came up with another way to explain things. It was a challenge when my mind was buzzing with sexual satisfaction. "What's the technical term for blow jobs?"

"Technical term?"

"Oral sex. Sex is in the name, right? Although I

guess I invalidated my point, since your dick was penetrating my mouth, didn't I? Oops."

That got him to grin. "In fairness, it's super hard to think right now."

"Then don't think." I curled up next to him, resting my head on his shoulder as I sprawled out on top of him. "Keep feeling good."

He brought his arms up to hug me against his chest. "I feel better than good. I feel *great*."

"So do I."

His contented sigh made me smile as I snuggled against him. I looked forward to showing him even more pleasure in the future, but it was enough for now that he understood it was possible to feel that way with a loving partner.

Chapter Nine

ELIAS

I WOKE up with our positions reversed. North was on his back, with me nestled against his side, my left arm and leg slung across him as I used his shoulder for a pillow. If he had been Will or Josh, I would have slunk away in fear of getting told off for being so clingy. But North had more than proved he was nothing like my cruel ex-boyfriends. I relaxed further against him, enjoying listening to the steady thrum of his heartbeat as he slept.

Prior to him, I had always been drawn to older guys because I thought they had their lives together and wouldn't play games with my heart. Yet, it was the man four years younger than me that seemed to have everything all figured out. I admired the way he said whatever was on his mind without second-guessing himself into inaction. He wasn't afraid to say he desired me, nor was he ashamed of me. For some strange reason, he liked me for me, damage and all.

We hadn't known each other a full week yet, but North already knew me better than Will or Josh had in the months I spent with them. He saw who I really was and didn't berate me for still being upset about losing Mom. He never criticized me for being stupid enough for getting involved with two awful men. Not only did he not blame me for what happened, he didn't want me to blame myself for it, either. All he wanted was for me to feel good and be happy.

The memory of how incredible his blow job had been flustered me. Will had given me a few but stopped when it was obvious I couldn't come from one. How could I when all he did was lick my shaft with disgust after forbidding me from coming in his mouth because that was gross? Josh had flat out refused to "service" me, yet both men had demanded them all the time. They complained if I wasn't enthusiastic enough about having the "honor" of being allowed to suck their dick and swallow their cum.

I *hated* giving them. Will constantly shoved my head down, and Josh gagged me because he liked how it felt. He insisted I had to be on my knees, whether he was standing or sitting. Remembering how he held me in place as he rammed his cock into my mouth hard and fast like he was filming an imaginary porn video made me sick. To add insult to injury, he'd come on my face if his violence caused my tears to fall. Compared to that, the rough sex had been less horrible to endure, although it left my ass sore for days afterward.

For me, there had been no pleasure in giving head or having sex with either of them. It was something I had endured because that was what being in a relationship with them meant. They both made me feel used and dirty, both during and after. I was permanently filled with dread about when it would happen again, and self-loathing for never standing up for myself. Part of me resented that they expected from me what they weren't willing to give in return. But I still sucked their dick, because as awful as it was, it was less traumatizing than getting yelled at for refusing.

But North hadn't seemed disgusted or bored when he went down on me; he had been rapturous with joy. It looked like he had been enjoying his favorite treat as he did everything in his power to make me have as fantastic a time as him. I had assumed he was a great actor until he showed me he had ejaculated from satisfying me.

I couldn't process that he loved blow jobs so much. Sure, I hadn't tortured him like Will and Josh had done to me, but how could sucking off someone else make you come? North insisted that if I felt good, he felt good, but that had never been part of the equation with my exes. It seemed like the worse I felt, the better the experience was for them. I didn't have sex with them because I enjoyed it; I did it because it was a requirement to date them. The closest thing to gratification for me was being relieved when they came fast and it was over quicker.

That was fine with them, but North was different. I wanted to make him feel as incredible as he made me feel. More than that, I dared to hope that maybe being with him would be enjoyable. He was a wonderful listener and respectful of my boundaries. If I told him to stop because something hurt, I trusted that he would. And if last night was any indication, he wouldn't shove his dick into me and pound me as hard as he could until he shot his load. He would probably take his time preparing me and ensure that he wasn't having all the fun.

I pictured him taking me gently, our bodies rocking as we moved together. He'd kiss me tenderly, murmuring sweet words to me as he brought me to the edge of pleasure. I'd lose myself in him, holding on to him as he sent me over the heights of ecstasy. The mental picture was enough to make me grow hard, the visual filling me with a need to find out if being with North would really be like that.

The smart thing to do would be to move away from him before my erection woke him up. But part of me wanted to know what he'd do when he discovered how turned on I was by the thought of being with him. It drove me to be bold as I trailed my hand from his shoulder and down his chest. When I glanced down, even without my glasses on, I snickered at the sight of a blurry yet distinctive tent in the blanket.

He wrapped his arm around my waist as he drew me closer. "Hmm?"

I couldn't help but tease him a little. "Do you wake up with morning wood every morning?"

"Only when I'm in bed with someone as gorgeous as you."

"How can you be that smooth when you're barely conscious?"

He chuckled as he pointed out, "You're acting like I'm the only one here with a dick as hard as a diamond."

"I didn't wake up this way, though."

"Oh, really?" I shivered as North trailed his fingers along my side. "Then what's got you so worked up this early in the morning?"

I shrugged, trying to play it casual. "I was just thinking."

"Thinking about what?"

Normally, I'd be too embarrassed to fess up to what I had been imagining, but I tried being brave. "Returning the favor from last night."

North rolled me onto my back as he propped himself up to look down at me with a serious expression, careful to stay where I could see him. "Elias, that wasn't a favor. That was something I freely did because I wanted to do it. I expect nothing in return.

You're never under any obligation to do anything to me you don't want to do, okay?"

His sincerity soothed my nervousness away. I reached up to draw him closer into an insistent kiss, needing him to understand what his reassurance meant to me. I had to know if I could derive pleasure from giving it to him. "Sorry, that came out wrong. I want to do the same thing to you, not because I think you expect it from me, but because I want to try."

He searched my gaze for a long moment. "If you change your mind and need to stop at any point, I promise I won't get mad at you."

His words made my heart clench in my chest as he addressed my unspoken concern. "How did you know that's what I needed to hear?"

"Because you look scared." He traced the outline of my jaw, his gentle touch easing the pit of tension in my stomach. "But you also look determined, which is why I'm not trying to talk you out of it. Just remember: if you're not enjoying it, I'm not either. If I'm right on the brink and you stop because you don't want me to come in your mouth, that's okay."

I kissed him with the full force of my gratitude, hoping he understood how much hearing that meant to me. He didn't resist as I eased him back, then moved to straddle myself over him. Unlike last time, fear didn't overcome me. I rubbed my hardness against his as I shifted forward and started trailing kisses down his neck. A breathy sigh escaped him as he acquiesced to my attention, tilting his head to give me better access. Rather than barking orders like my exes, he let me go at my own pace. I appreciated that he stroked my arm to reassure me I was doing fine because he knew I couldn't see his expression to judge.

When the normal barrage of complaints I was taking too long or doing it wrong didn't come, I felt safe enough to keep going. I was unhurried as I worked my way down his bare chest. The smooth expanse was an unfamiliar experience for me with a partner, since my ex-boyfriends had both been hairy. I liked how their hairiness was a mark of them being older, but I had never cared for how it felt under my tongue. Kissing their furry chests always made me feel like a cat trying to groom them, which was a far cry from sexy manliness.

As a result, exploring him with alternating kisses and licks as my hands roamed over his soft skin was an enjoyable experience for me. For something so simple, it was deeply erotic and comforting, not only because it felt good, but was a further reminder of having nothing in common with my exes. His nipples pebbled under my attention, and I teased one of them with my tongue until it was a hard peak. I gave it a tentative tug with my lips. Judging by how he groaned "*Yes*" and tightened his grip on my forearm, he liked it. I did it again, and his hips thrust against mine in search of friction.

I got my first glimmer of how wonderful being responsible for his pleasure could be. It pushed me to make things better for him, so I moved back and tossed off the covers to give myself more room to move. I kept kissing my way downward until I reached his thin happy trail. Following it with my fingers, I couldn't understand why that small bit of hair was so arousing. Why did I feel compelled to trace it with my tongue, making my cock ache for relief? It was another unexpected turn-on, since Will and Josh had both been so hairy that their happy trails were more like wild thickets in a dense forest.

Needing to build up some more courage before heading further south, I detoured to one of his sharp hip bones. Without understanding my urge, I lapped my tongue against the ridge.

Almost as a test, I continued lavishing it with attention and kisses to see if he would command me to do something less weird. But to my surprise, he merely tweaked his own nipple with a pleased rumble as he seemed to enjoy himself. It confused me enough that I had to speak. "Does this feel good?"

"Can't you see the precum on my dick?" He laughed but immediately stopped. "Shit, I forgot you probably can't see that without your glasses. Sorry, I wasn't trying to be an asshole, I just meant it should be obvious how much I'm enjoying myself."

I reached over and rubbed my thumb over the head of his cock, smearing the bead that had gathered on the tip. It baffled me; I hadn't done anything yet. "Even though I'm doing something as weird as kissing your hip bone?"

"Yes, because you're the one who is touching and kissing me all over, making me feel amazing. If hip bones are your thing, more power to you. I'm never going to complain about being the center of attention."

His answer compelled me to mirror my actions on his other one. As it had before, there was something about the rigidness of it that inexplicably turned me on, as did the fact that he was allowing me to do such a strange thing because he thought I enjoyed it. It made me realize he was serious about enjoying stuff because I did, even a weird hip bone.

It gave me the courage to continue. My nerves returned as I ran my fingers through his nest of dark hair, stopping just short of my goal. "Is this okay?"

"As long as it's what you want."

It was what I wanted, so I wrapped my hand around his length to stroke it. He inhaled sharply, then started chuckling when I moved closer to see what I was doing.

"Wow, how bad are your eyes?"

"I can't see your belly button from here." What I could see was all eight glorious inches of him, proudly standing at attention and loving every ounce of attention it was receiving from me. It inspired awe and nervousness in equal parts. My other partners had been smaller and hurt like hell, not to mention gagged me to the point of throwing up more than once. But North wasn't them; he wouldn't deliberately harm me. I needed to believe that.

Instead of laughing like I expected, he asked, "That's part of why you panicked when I requested you to get on top of me yesterday, wasn't it? You couldn't see my face to judge my reaction, so your anxiety told you to assume the worst."

I looked up at him in surprise, even though he was an indistinct blur. "I know it's stupid, but—"

"No, it's not stupid," he interrupted me. "If you've only dealt with assholes, you wouldn't have any reason to believe I was staring up at you in awe of how fucking gorgeous you are and how lucky I am. But please take my word for it when I tell you I was looking at you then and now as the single most beautiful person I have ever seen."

"I'm pretty sure that's Rune."

North sat up and guided me up close enough to see the sincerity in his blue eyes. "No, it's you. And I say that as a dude who has gotten off to Rune's elevator commercial more times than is acceptable when I'm friends with his boyfriend."

He wasn't the only one. "In your defense, his commercial is *super* sexy."

"Nothing is sexier than watching you enjoy yourself." He kissed me with a passionate plea to believe him. I gave myself over to him, letting his tongue explore my mouth with a teasing hint of possessiveness. My exes had both been terrible kissers, but North always sent a tingle through me that reached down to my toes when his lips claimed mine. "I used to think Callum was the luckiest guy on the planet for scoring Rune, but I've definitely stolen his title now thanks to you."

My heart swelled with affection for him. "You mean that."

"I really, *really* do."

After indulging in another lingering kiss, I felt brave enough to keep going. Since he had started with my thighs yesterday, I took a cue from him. I mirrored his actions of kissing up his inner thigh, running my hand along the outer side in tandem. His muscles bunched as he reacted to me, which was a nice physical confirmation of how affected he was by the smallest show of affection from me.

North spread his legs further apart as I neared his sac, taking away my normal claustrophobia in that position. He drew a shuddering breath when I sucked on it while teasing him with my tongue.

That earned me an enthusiastic "Fuck yeah!"

His verbal encouragement affected me so much I had to stroke my erection a few times for relief as I continued toying with him. For the first time, I experienced dual pleasure as I finally understood that inspiring him to moan was a huge turn-on for me.

Continuing up to his shaft, I held it steady while I

toyed with his balls using my other hand. I kept expecting him to order me to move on, but all he did was sing my praises about how fantastic everything was.

My stomach twisted with nerves when I focused on the tip, knowing I was about to take his length into my mouth. That was when my exes would force themselves as deep as they could, which was the least enjoyable part of it all. I reminded myself North wasn't them; he wouldn't do that to me.

Easing onto him, I let my tongue rub along the underside of his cock as he slid into me. Pausing less than halfway down, I braced for the rough assault to begin, but all he did was groan, "Fucking *yes*!"

Surprised that I still had total control of the situation, I cautiously began working him, taking him a little deeper with each bob of my head. I let my other hand wander up to run over his stomach, feeling his clenched muscles as he restrained himself from moving his hips. I relaxed when I realized he had no intention of forcing himself on me. Normally, I only had to keep my mouth open as my exes ravaged me, but now I was free to do as I pleased. I teased the tip before going down his length again. My gag reflex was very prone to triggering, so I was careful not to take him too far.

Despite not deep-throating him, North didn't seem to have a single complaint. As he became increasingly vocal, swearing with abandon about how good I was making him feel, I was so turned on that it hurt. I had to touch myself again for some relief, unable to believe how much his enjoyment was impacting my own.

When I hummed around him, I tensed when his hand rested on the back of my head. My panic was about to kick in, because that action always led to my exes brutally forcing me to gag on them. They never stopped until they came. However, North didn't guide me to take in more of him. He carded his fingers through my hair, caressing me as he moaned, "God, your mouth is fucking *magical*!"

I kept waiting for him to use his grip to force himself on me, but he continued petting me, soothing my fears at the same time. It amazed me he was still letting me do whatever I wanted. When he didn't steal control away from me, I gave in to his touch with a moan of my own. His gentleness combined with his soft cries inspired by me almost sent me to the brink.

It was because of me he was getting off. I was the one who was causing him to lose his mind as he sighed my name like it was the most sacred word in the English language. He was living for everything I was doing, grateful for the gift I was giving him, and never taking more than I offered. It was the first time I felt powerful in that position. Discovering pleasuring him *was* pleasurable for me was the most erotic and arousing realization I had ever had.

"Fuck, I'm so close, Elias! I can't hold out for

much longer." His fingers tightened in my hair, but it wasn't painful. All he was doing was warning me I was free to stop if I wanted to, letting me know that it was okay if I didn't want to keep going. He cared enough to not take me by surprise or force me to do something that, for all he knew, I hated doing.

It was that show of consideration that pushed me over the edge. I came all over my hand with a moan, triggering North's orgasm. He cried my name as his seed shot down my throat. It amazed me that at the apex of climax, he was still considerate enough not to shove himself deeper and gag me as he got off.

I let him fall free as I swallowed, wiping the corner of my lips with the back of my clean hand. My mind was a jumble of sexual gratification, shocked that giving him head had gotten me off. It was a relief that North had helped prove yet again that I had never been the problem like I had assumed for so many years. I was perfectly capable of enjoying pleasuring my partner and even getting off on it, which I hadn't thought possible. It was a stunning revelation that caused excitement to stir inside me that maybe sex with him would be a totally different and pleasurable experience, too.

"You doing okay over there?"

While I couldn't make out his face thanks to my poor eyesight, I heard the concern in his voice. It overwhelmed me he cared more about how I was doing than his own euphoria. I held up my hand as proof that I was more than fine. "Stunned but satisfied. *Wow*."

"That's fucking awesome!"

The sheer exuberance of his excitement for me made me laugh. In that moment, I was so light and free that I barely believed I was myself. "It really is."

North moved close enough to show me how happy he was for me. "I'm so proud of you."

Without me saying, he understood how momentous the experience had been for me. I melted into his kiss, flying high on the rush that being with him gave me. Even my most naïve dreams about what being with someone would be like hadn't been as satisfying as the reality of being with him. I had never been more grateful to be wrong in my entire life.

Chapter Ten

NORTH

AFTER MY ENJOYABLE wake-up call from Elias, he let me use his shower since I hadn't been home after coming over Friday. It was disappointing when he declined to join me, because I loved being wet and naked with a sexy guy. The main reason I hadn't insisted he change his mind was that I refused to be pushy or rush him into something he was uncomfortable with. It sounded like both of his ex-boyfriends had constantly done that to him, and I wasn't about to be the third asshole on that list.

The other benefit was I could jerk off to a fantasy of pleasuring him while surrounded by the scent of his incredible ocean-scented body wash. It made me want to make out with him on a beach after giving him a sensuous massage to put sunscreen all over him.

Once I got dressed, I found him at the kitchen table on his phone. He looked adorably preppy in a lavender polo and faded jeans. Since being bold had served me well so far, I bent down to give him a gentle, lingering kiss. It was a sweet, perfect moment that made me realize how hard and fast I was falling for Elias. Everything about him lit me up inside like a firework show on the Fourth of July. I craved him so much it would have scared me if he weren't so wonderful. "Good morning."

"Morning."

It was none of my business, but I couldn't help but notice the website on his phone screen. "Checking Signs of the Times?"

His faint blush was charming. "Yeah, sorry."

"Why sorry?"

"Because it's silly to read horoscopes."

I didn't like that he was sheepish about something that wasn't a problem. "You said it was your mom's thing, right?"

Elias rubbed the back of his hand as he glanced away from me. "She always checked them over breakfast because she enjoyed starting out her mornings with positivity and possibility. She got so excited whenever their predictions came true. I used to think it was ridiculous and hokey, but once she was gone, I missed her excitement about them. It probably sounds sad, but reading them every morning makes her feel closer."

I sat down next to him and guided him to look at me. "No, it's sweet."

"I'm sure they're written by some lady into healing crystals and mystic energy. It's illogical, but sometimes astrology has just enough accuracy to almost make me wonder, you know?"

Elias had no idea how far off base he was. The truth was, I had been writing the horoscopes on Signs of the Times for three years. My aunt was their IT manager, so she had recommended me for the position after their last person had to quit suddenly. Since one of my majors was creative writing, I decided it would be a fun part-time job. It was easy to forget that people read them and that they had a meaningful impact on them.

Refocusing my attention, I teased him, "Like predicting I would be a stranger who will change your life by bringing you a lifetime of love and happiness?"

The smile that tugged at the corner of his mouth was too precious. "Yeah."

"There's nothing wrong with finding comfort in horoscopes. Plenty of people do." Our millions of readers were a testament to that.

"Usually it's middle-age moms who complain about everything in their life being a mess because Mercury is in retrograde. When was the last time you met a guy my age who reads them regularly? It's embarrassing."

I reached out and took his hand into mine to give it a reassuring squeeze. "It's not, and I don't think any less of you because of it. If it comforts you because of your mom, then that's great. I'm glad you have something that can do that for you." It was nice knowing that even before I met him, I had been helping him.

"You don't think it's stupid?"

I chose my words carefully. "No, I don't. If nothing else, horoscopes are well-intentioned. If they encourage people to make positive changes in their lives or comforts them in darker times, then what's the harm?"

Elias's relief at my opinion was obvious. "Thank you. Red accidentally found out when I checked it at the bar once after a busy day when I hadn't been able to get to it in the morning. After that, he started asking about it every visit. Other than him, you're the only other person who knows."

I had a momentary debate about if I should tell him the truth about my part-time job writing the horoscopes he read. Lying to him by omission didn't sit well with me. However, I also didn't want to destroy the comfort Elias derived from them by shattering his illusion about them. If he didn't know it was me, I could start running encouraging ones for him whenever he was having a hard time. Secretly taking care of him was appealing and outweighed ruining something that meant so much to him.

"Thank you for telling me. You have nothing to be ashamed of, okay?"

He nodded, looking considerably less worried.

The best method to convince him was to show

interest. "So, what does yours say is in store for you today?"

It was a good sign that he didn't question my sincerity. He unlocked his phone and read the horoscope I had written. "If you want to learn more about someone, Virgo, you need to make an effort. Don't be afraid of what you might discover, unless you're scared of finding true love. Embracing everything about your special someone will bring you even closer together."

"I've gotta say, it sounds promising." Considering I always submitted my horoscopes a week ahead of time, my accuracy regarding us impressed me. "What about mine?"

"What's your sign?"

I couldn't hold in my laughter. "Did you just use a cheesy hippy pickup line on me?"

His giggle was so cute I wanted to kiss him and taste his delight. "I guess I did."

"What sign do you think I am?"

Elias mulled it over before guessing, "You seem like a Leo, but you also radiate some serious Aries energy, as Mom would say."

"Yet again, Genevieve continues to be shockingly accurate about me."

I was glad that made him happy instead of sad. "It shouldn't surprise me at this point. When were you born?"

"April first."

Elias's incredulous expression was adorable. "Seriously?"

"Yep, Mom had a blast fucking with the staff at the hospital by playing an April Fools' trick on them. She acted shocked to discover she was pregnant with twins and not suffering from terrible indigestion and bloating. She kept insisting those weren't twin babies, it was the burrito and chimichanga she ate the night before coming back with a vengeance."

Elias laughed so hard that he had to wipe away tears of mirth. "You can't be serious!"

I grinned at him. "Oh, I absolutely am. They showed her sonograms with us, and she accused *them* of playing an April Fools' Day prank on *her* with fake pictures from some other lady. Mom used to do theatre in college, so she is a *very* good actress. She can play the indignant and outraged lady to perfection, so she had them fully convinced she was a looney nut."

"What about your dad?"

"When she said her water broke, he assumed she was pranking him. Mom's known for that kind of fuckery, so I can't blame him for not believing her. He tried calling her bluff by driving her to the hospital and was quite surprised she was in labor for real."

Elias's gray eyes were as wide as saucers. "Your family sounds wild."

"Oh, we're that and then some. When the nurse asked what our names would be, Mom replied Sopaipillas and Churro, which apparently sent the woman to the edge. When Mom finally said North and West Easton, the nurse stormed out of the room in anger over being messed with. Dad had to chase her down and insist they were serious about our real names and beg her to fill out the official paperwork."

"That poor nurse!"

"The story has a happy ending. Mom apologized by having a catered lunch and ginormous cake delivered for the staff with 'Happy April Fools' Day' written on it. Once they recovered from the shock, they all had a good laugh."

Elias marveled at me in wonder. "That's the most absurd thing I've ever heard."

"Mom had been going stir-crazy on bed rest, so she got carried away after being cooped up too long with nothing to do. She wanted to tell them to name my sister Kviiilyn to really fuck with them, but she couldn't make a worthy male equivalent."

"How would being named Kaitlyn mess with them?"

"Because she wasn't going to spell it any of the normal ways. She was going to spell it K-v-i-i-i-l-y-n."

Elias looked baffled. "Wait, how does that spell Kaitlyn? Wouldn't it be Kay-vee-iii-lyn or something?"

"Because the v-i-i-i are the Roman numerals for the number eight, so it would be Kay-eight-lyn. Well, technically it would be Kay-octo-lyn if it was *real*

Roman numerals, but Mom never lets details like that stop her harebrained plans."

He cracked up, making me grin at how amused he was. "That's even more absurd than pretending to name your kid *Sopaipillas*! Where did she come up with that?"

"That's just how Mom's brain works. We're lucky she hadn't heard of Abcde, or I might have been stuck with that one and my sister really would be Kviiilyn."

"Absidee?"

"It's spelled A-b-c-d-e but pronounced Ab-si-dee. It made the news a few years ago, and Mom lamented for *weeks* she didn't think of it first. She joked about having another set of twins so she could pull off the ultimate name prank, but that's impossible while Dad is busy playing with penguins."

I couldn't blame Elias for looking baffled. "Is he a zookeeper?"

It was such a pure guess that I had to smile. "No, he's down in Antarctica."

Elias looked like he wasn't sure if he should believe me or not. "Are you serious? Why would your dad be in *Antarctica*?"

"He's a scientist researching global warming, so he lives down there for several months out of the year. He used to live up at the North Pole when he conducted research, but I think he transferred to stop Mom from joking she married Santa. Getting ribbed about not bringing her a pet penguin home is a lot less embarrassing."

Elias shook his head in amazement. "Wow, that's quite the story. I see why you're an author."

"It's all a hundred percent true, which is the most unbelievable thing of all." I wasn't unaware of the fact that I always sounded like I was lying out of my ass whenever I told stories of my family lore. I had an idea, but I needed to get us back on track to make it happen. "So, what does my horoscope say?"

He unlocked his phone again and pulled up my page to read from. "If you *really* want to have fun, Aries, now is the time to let someone into your life. Let them see the real you. If it's meant to be, they'll love you for you and not go screaming for the hills."

I tapped my chin as I pretended to consider something. "Well, if I'm supposed to let you into my life by showing you the real me, and you're supposed to make an effort to learn more about me, visiting my mom's house would be a perfect solution."

"After hearing that story, I'm not sure if I'm prepared for that."

"In fairness, no one is *ever* ready to meet my mom. She's a lot of everything, but in a good way. West will also be around since its Sunday family dinner night. I'd love if you'd join us." I hoped he'd agree, because I wasn't willing to give up my time with him yet.

"Do they know who I am?"

I chuckled at the notion of my mother and twin

being uninformed about any part of what was going on in my world. "Not to weird you out, but there's no such thing as a secret in my family. We're *very* open. Probably *too* open if I'm being honest. However, Dad was the only one of us who was born with a filter, so there's no helping it. We're impulsive and say whatever is on our minds, even if it's 'Holy shit, I found the love of my life' after a single dinner together."

Elias flushed a beautiful scarlet as he tightened his grip on my hand. "You actually feel that way?"

"Chalk it up to chaotic Aries energy from an April Fools' baby," I said with a shrug. "It may not make sense, it may be too fast, but fuck if I care about anything other than being happy with you. Whether I fell in love with you in three months, three days, or three seconds, the result will always be you're the one my heart wants."

"But I'm supposed to be a levelheaded Virgo. What's my excuse for feeling the same way?"

"Because I'm amazing," I answered with a charming grin.

When he let go of my hand, I worried for a moment that I had overstepped. To my surprise, he straddled himself over my lap, looping his arms around my neck. "You certainly are."

I cupped his ass to guide him closer for a kiss. He laced his fingers through my hair as he opened for me to explore his wet warmth with my tongue. I could enjoy him every day for a million years and I'd still beg for another million more. While I wasn't a true believer, I thanked the cosmic universe that had granted me the wisdom to write the perfect Virgo horoscope for the night we met.

When we parted, Elias licked his lips to catch the last taste of me. "Okay."

His kiss distracted me. "Okay?"

"As in, okay, I'd like to go with you tonight, unless you've changed your mind."

My heart overflowed with joy. "Of course I haven't. I'd love to take you home. And I'm not saying that because it means I can change into different clothes, so you see I own more than two outfits."

His light laughter filled me with a warm glow of contentment as I fell for him all over again. Who knew being in love was so fucking awesome?

Chapter Eleven

ELIAS

EVERYTHING ABOUT NORTH was unexpected and borderline unbelievable, so it shouldn't have surprised me that his family owned a talking cat. Woof greeted us at the door, a beautiful lilac point Siamese wearing a blue bow tie. He sat down, wrapping his tail around himself as he looked up and meowed hello.

"Hey, Woofie. How's it going?"

The cat's next meow was lengthier, almost sounding like a baby crying as he warbled.

"Yeah, I hear you. But at least your bow tie is cute?" I stared in amazement as Woof drew himself up to his full height and showed it off. "Go meet Elias."

On command, Wolf came over to me and looked up with beautiful blue eyes. He sniffed in my direction, his tail flicking as he silently assessed me. I crouched down to introduce myself. "Nice to meet you, Woof. I'm Elias."

He butted his head against my hand, accepting scritches behind the ear from me with a loud murffle. He continued allowing me to fawn over him, which I was all too happy to do since I loved cats and rarely got to spend time around them.

"Aren't you handsome? I know someone who would be very envious of your bow tie."

"Oh, you're right. Callum would love it." North pulled out his phone. "Woof, it's picture time! Strike a pose, buddy."

To my astonishment, the cat took a few steps away and sat down while looking up expectantly at the camera.

"Another stellar shot. Callum's going to adore you."

I swore he preened at the praise as he continued chattering and rubbing against North's legs.

"Yeah, that's totally worth a treat. Come on." He walked toward the kitchen with the cat trotting along at his side and me following behind them.

I cast covert looks around the home, decorated with an eclectic collection of art. I wondered if any of it was North's work, but I had a more pressing question. "Why didn't you mention you had a talking cat?"

He laughed as he opened a drawer and pulled out a bottle of treats. Woof stood up on his hind legs and pawed to get at them. "Sorry, I forget that normal people don't have entire conversations with their cats. He's special that way."

"That's amazing."

North shook out some treats and crouched down so Woof could have them. "He's a prissy little thing, though. He won't eat a treat if you put it on the floor. It's too plebeian for him or something. Right, Woof?"

The cat murmured an affirmative as he continued crunching on the hard treats.

North patted him on the head. "You're such a good boy."

Woof waved his tail in the air as he looked up with an expression that haughtily said, *Of course I am*.

After he finished, North stood up and washed his hands. "Okay, bud, we're going upstairs. I'll let you know what Callum says about your bow tie later, okay?"

The cat trilled as he walked into the living room and crawled into a giant banana bed to take a nap.

"He's incredible," I commented in awe. "I've never seen such a chatty cat before."

"Siamese are notorious talkers, but he's something else." North gestured for me to follow him. "You should hear him, Mom, and West carry on with each other."

I could only imagine. "While we're here, can I see Gary?" That was the name of the dragon he had made of soda flip tabs. The picture had been amazing, but I was excited to appreciate the details of the actual sculpture.

"No, he's at my apartment, taking up way too much space in my room. I'd be happy to show him to you there, though." After we entered his bedroom, North shut and locked his door behind us. I arched an eyebrow at him in silent question, causing him to grin. "You'll understand when West gets here. She thinks being three minutes and thirty-six seconds older than me gives her the right to barge in whenever she pleases. You'd think catching me jerking off so many times would stop that habit but nope."

I blushed at the thought of getting caught pleasuring myself. "I'd die of embarrassment if that happened to me."

"Welcome to the joys of having a sister who doesn't believe in personal boundaries," North said with a laugh as he opened his closet. "Besides, it's not like I haven't gotten payback."

"What do you mean?"

He smirked at me as he pulled off his shirt, giving me a whole new reason to feel flushed. "Oh, I've had a lot of fun at her expense. My favorite was when I got into bed with her boyfriend while she used the bathroom." He took off his pants next, then his underwear. I tried and failed to not to stare at his beautiful body. "He was a homophobic dick, so I enjoyed shattering his bullshit illusions about himself."

"How?"

North slid on new rainbow tie-dye boxers with the closest thing to a sheepish expression I had seen from him. "I might have aroused him while he thought I was my sister because I was convinced his homophobia stemmed from an unwillingness to accept his own sexuality. Maurilio was a jock who tried *way* too hard to be straight. I wanted to open his eyes a little."

"You messed around with your sister's boyfriend?" I asked in shock.

"No, I kept my hands above the waistband with just touching to prove a point to him. When she returned from the bathroom, she pouted that when she imagined a threesome with two men in her bed, I wasn't involved."

The reaction boggled my mind. "She wasn't mad at you?"

"Nah, she thought it was hilarious."

"What about him?"

North grinned as he slipped on a pair of skinny jeans that hugged his ass in a distracting way. "Maurilio learned some important lessons about himself that morning. Mercifully, he didn't deck me for it."

"Is she with him now?" It unsettled me he might still be around.

"No, but they're good friends."

I couldn't understand how that was possible. "Did they break up because of that incident?"

North put on a mesh button-down T-shirt covered

in beautiful blue floral embroidery. "No, she was sick of the shitty sex and ended it shortly afterward, but not before convincing him to get over his hang-ups so he could be happy. Thankfully, he listened. Maurilio's engaged to his best friend, Brad, and couldn't be happier. He asked her to be one of his groomsmen in the wedding, so they're cool."

It was hard not to get distracted by his nipples peeking out from behind the embroidered flowers. "That's nice."

North pulled me into an embrace. "I was dumb, single, and in high school when that happened. I'd never do that now, especially not when I'm with you."

His reassurance made me realize how worried I must have looked. "He could have hurt you for doing that."

"Yeah, and I would have deserved it," North said with an unconcerned shrug. "But Maurilio was all bark and fucking miserable in the closet, which made my sister unhappy. In my immature mind, I was doing them both a favor. I tried to apologize to him for it, but he thanked me later for helping him. Once he overcame the bigoted fears he inherited from his religious father, he turned out to be a cool dude. It's all good now. He's out and proud, West is having fun living life to the fullest, and I'm the luckiest guy of all time to be with you. You have nothing to worry about. I only have eyes for you, Elias."

Hearing him reaffirm his commitment to me helped soothe my concerns but didn't erase them. "Even though I'm boring?"

"You're many things, but definitely not boring." North interrupted my next protest with an insistent kiss as he backed me up against his desk. "Plus, I have plenty of Aries chaos for us both."

"That's true."

"Your Virgo calm and stability will keep me from losing control." He started kissing his way up my neck, so I tilted my head to give him better access. "Although, I'd love to lose control right now and fucking ravage you."

Part of me was more than ready to invite him, especially as I gave in to the temptation to brush my thumbs against his exposed nipples through the embroidered mesh. The feeling of them hardening excited me while he passionately kissed me, pressing me hard against the desk as he rocked his hips against me. Freezing water doused my arousal when his doorknob rattled. A woman's voice called out from the other side, "Do you think a locked door is going to stop me from getting a peek at your new beau?"

He stepped back with a sigh, just in time for his lock to get picked and door to swing open.

A triumphant female version of North crowed at her victory. Her hair was white with streaks of pastel blue, purple, and pink running through it as an iridescent effect. She wore a stunning pink-and-purple patchwork overbust corset with a black lace purple skirt. It paired nicely with black boots trimmed with military gold accouterments. Her purple-and-silver ombre glitter eyeshadow was theatrical and beautiful, further accentuated by her metallic black, blue, and purple shimmer lipstick that drew attention to her full lips. Even her black holo nails matched. She looked like a badass heroine who had stepped out from a steampunk fantasy novel. "I don't know why you bothered locking your door at all. That puny thing never stops me. That wouldn't give you enough time to get your clothes back on."

"And yet we're dressed."

"Unfortunately," she retorted with a cheeky grin and a wink in my direction that brought heat to my cheeks once more.

North gestured at his sister. "Elias, this is my twin, West. West, this is Elias. Keep your smart-ass comments and hands to yourself."

I extended my hand to her. "Hi, it's nice to meet you."

Rather than accepting, West tugged me into a tight hug as she squealed, "Oh, you're so cute! Look at you! You have *manners*!"

I returned the embrace because I didn't know what else to do.

She stepped backward and held my face in her

hands as she assessed me. Her eyes had more green in them than North's, but the twins looked remarkably similar despite her dyed hair and dramatic makeup. She must have liked whatever she saw because she lit up with a pleased grin. "Well done, brother. I can't believe you found a keeper."

The question was out of my mouth before I could stop it. "What makes you think I'm a keeper?"

"A twin knows these things," she cryptically said, reminding me of how mysterious her brother had seemed in the bar when I first met him. "Wow, I'm impressed, North. You actually fell for a great guy. Thanks for making sure he's cute. I'll never tire of looking at this gorgeous face at our weekly dinners."

I wasn't sure how to respond to that, but she had no problem keeping the one-sided conversation going by herself. "Welcome to the family, handsome." It stunned me when she pressed a kiss against my cheek. I could only blink at her when she said in a singsong voice, "Mom is gonna *love* him."

"Where is she, anyway?" North asked.

Before West could answer, Woof entered the room, his tail waving high in the air with a curled-over kink in a question mark. He meowed as if he was making an announcement, causing West to giggle.

She scooped him up, rubbing his belly as she cooed, "Who's Mommy's cute little minion? You are!"

I had never seen a cat look more indignant. He

fussed at the treatment and struggled to get free without success.

"Okay, okay. Go tell Mom we're on our way down."

As soon as West set Woof down, he sauntered out of the room with a flicker of his tail and headed downstairs at a dignified pace. I could only presume he was following orders, because that's how weird everything was at that point.

The three of us followed the cat, with my nerves starting to catch up with me over meeting North's mother. I had never met my boyfriend's parents before, so it was unfamiliar territory for me. After hearing so many wild stories about his mom, Linda, I wasn't sure what I was in store for. North holding my hand helped settle some of my nervousness.

Whatever I had been expecting, a petite blond woman with rainbow highlights in a bob cut wasn't it. She was beautiful in her white dress with a blue, red, and purple geometric square pattern, which was short in the front and longer in the back. Even if she were wearing heels, she would have been shorter than all of us. She had a youthful vibrance that made it impossible to guess her age. At present, she was praising her cat for a job well done, fluffing up his cheeks and cooing at him. "Such a wonderful little Woofie. Mommy had West make you a new crown. Are you excited?"

Once again, Woof meowed like he understood her question.

"All your fans are going to love this!"

"Fans?" I accidentally asked in confusion.

Linda looked up at me, her expression lighting up when she saw me. It was easy to see the family resemblance between her and her children in her beautiful smile and lovely features. She chided her cat, "Woof, why didn't you mention Elias was here?" When her only answer was a flick of his tail, she returned her attention to me. She came around the kitchen counter and cupped my cheeks the same way West had. "Oh, would you look at you? Adorable!"

"Thank you."

Her squeal of delight sounded like her daughter's. "And he has *manners*!"

That she had also called out my manners over a basic politeness confused me. "Is that unusual?"

"Have you ever met a frat boy with manners?" Linda asked with a laugh.

It made me wonder how many frat boys North had dated in the past. "I can't say I've met any. That wasn't my scene."

North and West simultaneously said, "You're not missing much."

It was an interesting glimpse of their twin bond, especially when they were standing next to each other. If he wore a wig and a dress, he'd look identical to his sister.

"I kept to myself during undergrad and law school." Minus the part where I got tangled up with Will in the beginning of college, but I didn't say that out loud.

"It's amazing you're already an attorney when you're so young!" Linda gushed. "You two could learn something from him about being studious."

"Oh, yeah, because I'm *such* a slacker with a double major and a part-time job as an author," North retorted.

West rolled her eyes at her brother. "Don't act like you're the only one pulling that off. My double major of fashion design and photography while balancing an internship is just as much of a pain in the ass, if not more so. You wouldn't last five minutes working for Kalindi."

"Hey, give me *some* credit. I'd probably manage to be charming for at least seven minutes before she threw something at me."

The uncommon name rang a bell for me. "Do you mean Kalindi Urslana?"

West's excitement was palpable. "Yeah! Do you know her?"

"Not personally, but she was my mom's favorite designer." She was practically all my mother wore. Her closet was stuffed with that designer's clothes, because neither Dad nor I had gone through her things. We weren't quite there yet. "You work for her?"

"I had an internship with her this summer. I must have done something right, because she offered to extend it into a full year. It's amazing, considering most of her interns don't even make it a week."

Unaware of anything other than the designer's name, I asked, "Is she hard to work for?"

"She's a demanding perfectionist, but you don't reach her level without having exacting standards. The experience has taught me what to do when I have my own atelier someday and, more importantly, what *not* to do."

"And I get the benefit of her employee discount," Linda said as she did a spin in her cute dress.

West snorted at that. "Yeah, like you need it."

"Hey, even if I can afford full price, I appreciate an excellent bargain." She gestured at herself grandly. "The tragedy is that I look this amazing when I work from home."

"What do you do?" I asked, since North had never mentioned what she did for a living.

"I'm an author."

Before I could ask for details, West provided them. "Not just any author. She's Arrietty Quenby."

My jaw dropped in shock. "*Seriously?*"

"You've heard of me?" Linda acted surprised, as if Arrietty Quenby wasn't one of the most famous living fantasy authors today.

It took a moment for me to find my voice. "Of

course I have! We have all of your books. *Mistress of Nothing, Master of All* was Mom's all-time favorite. I've lost count of how many times I've read *The Prince's Thief*, because I love it so much."

"Riston and Hedley were something special, weren't they?" Linda sighed happily. "I miss writing them. They were such a sweet couple, considering their relationship started with a stabbing."

I had to laugh at that. Stabbing aside, seeing the romantic bond between the two men had helped me realize why I needed to break up with Will when I was a freshman in college. But that detail was a little too personal to share. Instead, I settled for saying, "That book really means a lot to me."

"Aww, I'm so happy to hear that!" Linda gave me a big hug, before looping her arm around me to pull me closer. She gave her son a warning look. "North, don't screw this up. I want to keep this cutie pie forever, got it?"

I blushed from the implication, making everyone laugh. It was strange being the center of attention of three extroverts when I was such an introvert, but their warmth kept it from being uncomfortable. I was still curious about my unanswered question from earlier. "Are your readers fans of Woof?" I had never been active on social media, so I was unaware of her online presence.

"Many of them are, but he has his own fans! I

dress up our darling boy in costumes that West makes for him."

"Does that mean she also made the costume from the picture you showed me of him with the crown and cape?" I asked North.

West answered for him. "Yep! Making them for him is great practice. Oh, that reminds me! I'll be right back."

After West left to grab her bag, Linda tapped the kitchen island as she commanded, "Woofie, up!"

To my amazement, he obeyed by jumping up, purring over being rewarded with pets.

West returned with a large metallic silver box. It almost reminded me of the one my mom had used for my birthday present. She set it on the counter before opening it to remove what was inside. "Ta-da!"

She revealed an impressive blue flower crown with sparkling red berries. Each of them was different, but they were all gorgeous.

Linda applauded her daughter's work. "Oh, that's beautiful, honey!"

Woof walked over to her and sat in front of her expectantly. She held it up to him for his sniff of approval before putting it on him. Then she pulled out a blue rhinestone collar and put it around his neck as the final touch. It glittered in the kitchen light as he regally posed.

The most amazing thing of all was that he didn't

remove the crown off his head. Instead, he went over to Linda next.

"Such a pretty prince!" She scratched under his chin, earning a happy trill for her efforts. "West, you've outdone yourself!"

"Can you call it a crown without every inch being covered in glitter?" North joked, getting punched hard in the arm by his sister for his comment. He rubbed his bicep with a scowl. "Ow, what was that for?"

"For being a smart-ass," West and her mom said together, before they both laughed. Linda added, "Woof, go show North your glitter berries."

Once again, he did as commanded, walking over to stand in front of North, who was snickering about glitter berries.

"Yes, very nice, Woofie," he complimented, giving him a fond scratch behind the ear.

"For your information, I *wanted* to do flowers made entirely out of glitter, but the fallout was too messy," West said with a scowl. "I got in trouble last time for the glitter crown making a mess, so I was *trying* to be thoughtful this time. Besides, the blue flowers bring out his eyes, don't you agree?"

Linda walked over and gave her daughter a hug. "You did a wonderful job, sweetie. Woof couldn't ask for a better stylist and designer than you. Did you bring your camera so we can take pictures while dinner is in the oven?"

"I never go anywhere without it!"

Their mom turned her attention toward me. "How does lasagna sound to you, Elias?"

"Delicious."

She beamed with pleasure. "Marvelous! Let's get that started, and then we'll start our photo shoot."

North came over and murmured for my ears only, "Doing okay?"

Mindful to keep my voice down as she began prepping dinner, I asked, "Why didn't you warn me your mom was Arrietty Quenby?" That was a hell of a thing to be broadsided with.

"Were you already nervous about meeting her?"

"Yeah."

He grinned. "Wouldn't you have been more nervous if you knew who she was?"

"Good point." I never would've had the courage to come over if I had known I'd be having dinner with one of my favorite authors. Once again, I had to question the coincidence that made me wonder if maybe my mother was getting her laughs in the afterlife.

"You'll be fine. She loves you already." North gave me a quick kiss to reassure me, checking how we could help.

Linda gave us our tasks for prepping the lasagna, which was something I was more than comfortable with after years of helping my mom cook. It was fun watching as they laughed and joked with each other. I also appreciated how they included me in on their banter, which made me feel less like an outsider. At the same time, the loving familial bond between a mother and her children intensified that ever-present ache that I never seemed to escape. I tried my best to fight against it, but my pain encroached on my enjoyment of being part of a warm family.

With a massive effort, I held it together long enough to finish dinner prep and watch the beginning of Woof's photo shoot. I excused myself to their purple dining room to regain my composure in private. The white bay window let in light, giving an airy atmosphere, which was further enhanced by the glass table trimmed with white wood. Elegant lavender-and-white chairs surrounded the table, with a stunning crystal chandelier hanging above it that sent fractured rainbow lights on the walls. There also was a large cutout wall clock with Roman numerals and a compass in the center. It was a spectacular room that my mother would have loved, since purple was her favorite color and interior decorating was one of her passions.

Burning tears gathered that I fought hard to not let fall. It was so frustrating to be having fun one minute and then feel like I was going to shatter from grief the next. I hated being envious of North and West for having such an amazing mother alive and well when mine was no longer with us. I would have given anything to see her again and tell her how unbelievable it was that my boyfriend's mother was one of our favorite authors. She would have laughed until she couldn't breathe and then laughed some more. Without a doubt, she would have invited herself over and become best friends with Linda. The two of them would have delighted in seeing their sons in love together. Knowing Mom, they would've had our entire wedding planned before the end of their first meeting.

I looked up at the crown molding on the ceiling as I focused on breathing and not letting my grief get the best of me. When I heard footsteps coming closer, I assumed it would be North checking on me. Instead, Linda approached with a sympathetic expression that said without words she understood what I was going through. She held her arms out to me and gave the kind of hug that only moms could give. It pushed me right to the edge of being overcome by my hurt. I caved to my emotions when she softly told me, "It's okay to still miss your mom."

Linda was shorter than my mother and smelled of sunshine and flowers instead of citrus and rich woods, but she offered me the same understanding embrace that mine had. I surrendered to my tears, embarrassing as it was. I took off my glasses as she stroked my hair the way Mom always had and let me feel without judgment. She shushed my apologies as I held her. "It's okay, sweetheart. I know it hurts."

After I had cried myself out, I lingered in her

embrace a moment longer, not ready to give up her motherly comfort yet. But then my embarrassment kicked in that I had just sobbed on one of my favorite author's shoulder and the mother of my boyfriend I wanted to impress. I reluctantly pulled back to wipe away the tear streaks from my cheeks and put my glasses on. "I'm so sorry, I'm—"

She finished my sentence for me in a gentle voice. "Still grieving. The first year is the hardest. Trust me, I've been there. I was a wreck after I lost my father when I wasn't much older than you."

"Does it ever get better?"

"Gradually, although that's a pain that will ache from time to time when you least expect it. Be kind to yourself and give yourself the space to grieve. Don't be like me and bottle it up inside. That leads to a messy implosion further down the road that makes it worse. One of the best pieces of advice I ever received was treat yourself the way you would your friend."

I sniffled as I turned her words over in my mind. "Meaning, if I wouldn't berate my friend for being sad after losing their mom less than a year ago, I shouldn't do it to myself?"

"Exactly. Use that beautiful kindness in your heart on yourself for once. You deserve it."

No wonder North was so wise. "I'm trying hard not to be embarrassed right now."

"What's embarrassing about being a wonderful son who loves his mother?"

I smiled at her words. "But I wanted to make a good first impression."

"Honey, you did that before you stepped foot in this house."

That confused me. "How?"

"You made my son realize there's something more important than, 'Holy hell, he's *hot*,' for starters."

I covered my mouth to hold in a laugh at her accurate mimicry of North.

She gave me a cheeky grin before continuing. "You're also the only person he has introduced to me and West. That tells me he thinks you're worth all the teasing that we're going to dish out. Even if he doesn't say it, I can promise you he is head over heels for you. I can't tell you how glad I am that he let his heart fall in love instead of thinking only with his dick. West and I would have killed him if he brought home an insufferable frat boy to spend the rest of his life with."

My eyes must have been wide as saucers in shock, because Linda laughed. "Oops, sometimes I forget myself. If you ever wondered where North's lack of a filter came from, it's from my side of the family. Sorry about that."

It got a chuckle out of me, the heavy blanket of my grief starting to lift. "No, I appreciate it. Mom always spoke her mind, so I miss that honesty."

"Thank god, because you're in for a lifetime of it

from us. Whenever it gets to be too much, you can commiserate with my poor husband when he comes back from freezing his nuts off at the South Pole."

Linda reminded me of my mother in all the best ways. "I can't believe he's really in Antarctica."

"I'm still annoyed he kiboshed all my fun jokes about being Mrs. Claus when he moved down there. The least he could do is bring me a cute baby penguin in apology. And he had the nerve to tell me that there's not a gift shop in Antarctica, can you believe it?"

It drew another laugh from me. "It's the most believable thing I've heard all day, considering you have a talking cat, you're one of my favorite authors, and North told me about your ultimate April Fools' Day prank at the hospital."

She smirked at the latter example. "It was one of my finer moments, if I do say so myself."

"I should have known your real life would be extraordinary given how incredible your books are."

"Oh, if you think mine are great, read North's sometime." I remembered him mentioning he wrote erotica, so I hadn't expected his mother to read his sexy books. "I taught him everything he knows, and the brat will repay me someday by becoming more famous than me." She radiated motherly pride rather than actual annoyance.

Unsure of how much longer we could talk in private, it was important for me to say, "Thank you for being so understanding earlier. Letting that out really helped, even though I feel awful for crying on such a pretty and expensive dress."

She patted my cheek with a fond smile. "You have my permission to not feel bad for one more second about that, okay? Your feelings are far more important than a piece of fabric that will dry."

I nodded in agreement, letting her approval absolve me of my guilt.

"Oh, and one more thing. Remember: mom hugs are always free, welcomed, and encouraged."

Her warmth gave me the courage to be brave enough to take her up on that offer by hugging her again. "Thank you, Linda."

"Anytime, honey. And if North is ever a shithead, tell me, and I'll help you get him straightened out." I laughed at her impish grin. "Speaking of him, let's go see how West kept him from coming over here. Want to place bets on her restraint method? Because I'm thinking she had to hog-tie him to keep him down that long."

"Maybe sitting on him?"

We returned to the living room, where West was triumphantly pinning her brother on the floor by sitting cross-legged on his back. When he tried to buck her off, she flicked his ear, laughing when he hissed in pain.

"Thanks, honey. You did a great job," Linda praised her daughter. "Elias gets extra dessert for correctly guessing how you won the battle against your brother."

"Hey! Have a little sympathy for me," North grumbled.

"If you want sympathy, it's between 'sweat' and 'syphilis' in the dictionary, sweetie."

I stifled a laugh at Linda's retort, which was twice as funny to me considering how sympathetic she had been to me when we talked in the dining room.

"I'll let you up if you admit I'm the best," West taunted.

"Then I'll be here forever, because Elias is by far the best here."

West giggled as she moved off her brother. "That's fair. Go give your cute boyfriend a kiss and I'll forgive you for being such a dick."

The instant he was free, North scrambled away before his sister could change her mind. He hugged me like we had been apart for months instead of minutes. Concern was written all over his face. "Are you okay?"

I melted into his hug, wondering how I had found a magical family where everything impossible was true. "Yeah, I'm great."

North caressed my cheek as he kissed me sweetly on the lips.

His sister catcalled us, while Linda teased, "You call that a kiss? What kind of romance author are you? You can do better than that!"

"I could, but then we'd miss your delicious dinner," he retorted.

As if on cue, the oven beeped to signal the lasagna was ready. I squeezed North's hand as he held mine while leading me over to the kitchen. I hadn't realized how much I had missed being happy around family, but it was the best feeling in the world to be a part of that again.

Chapter Twelve

NORTH

I HAD BEEN CONCERNED when Elias returned from his talk with Mom looking as if he had been crying, but he had insisted everything was fine. It was amazing watching him open up and find a place within my family, but I still worried that maybe it was too much too fast for him.

When it came time to leave, my sister hugged him hard as he laughed. "Please tell me you're coming back soon!"

"We'd love if you'd join us for dinner next Sunday if we haven't sent you screaming for the hills yet," Mom added.

I held my breath as I waited for his answer. He was so precious as he shyly said, "I'd enjoy that if it's not too much trouble, but I don't want to impose."

"You have a standing invitation to come over whenever you want."

West released her hold on him. "Mom means it, too. We'd love to have you over, even if North isn't here."

"Really?"

"We joke about a lot of things, but definitely not about that," I told him. It was very apparent to me that they were so charmed by him they'd take his side over mine about everything. Given what a dumbass I could be from time to time, I wouldn't blame them for choosing him over me.

"How does champagne chicken sound?" Mom asked him.

"I've never had it before, but it sounds good."

West cheered at next week's dinner choice. "Oh, that's one of my favorites! You'll love it, Elias, I promise. I'll make that chocolate peanut-butter cheesecake we talked about earlier."

"Then I'll definitely be here if it's okay with North." He glanced in my direction with a hopeful look.

"It's more than okay with me. We'll be here."

"Should I bring anything?"

Mom shook her head. "Just your sweet self."

West hugged me with a squeal, before she said for my ears only, "Please don't fuck this up, North. I *really* like him. Like, 'can't wait to watch you walk down the aisle with him so we can spend every weekly dinner and holiday together forever' like him."

It thrilled me to hear that my sister was already enamored enough with him to imagine our future in the long term. "That makes two of us."

"You mean three of us," West reminded me with a giggle. "I'm pretty sure Mom's going to file the adoption papers as soon as you're out the door."

I checked to see his reaction to her pronouncement, but Mom was hugging him and privately telling him something. Curiosity burned inside of me when it made him hug her tighter with a beautiful smile as he thanked her again for everything.

"God, he's *so* fucking gorgeous."

For a moment I almost thought I had said that out loud but realized West had verbalized what I was thinking instead. "Yeah, he is."

"It's a pity he doesn't have a twin. Then we could have one of those weird twins-marrying-twins weddings."

Elias dashed her hopes. "Sorry, I'm an only child. My closest cousin lives in Vancouver and is already married with kids."

West playfully pouted. "Damn it!"

We all laughed as we exchanged our last goodbyes and hugs before Elias and I left. In the light of the full moon, his white-blond hair gave him an ethereal beauty that made my heart stutter in my chest. He was so perfect I almost couldn't believe that he was real and reciprocated my feelings.

Once we were in the car, I turned to him as I asked, "Was that okay? I realize we're a lot, but—"

To my surprise, he silenced me with a tender kiss that melted my insides into mush. He held my gaze as he said with the utmost sincerity, "Thank you, North."

"For what?"

"For letting me come over here tonight and reminding me of how good it feels to be part of a happy family."

I wanted to hug him, but our positions in the car made it too difficult. Instead, I settled for caressing his cheek, loving when he leaned into my touch. "They weren't joking about adopting you. Mom and West love you enough that they'll keep you and boot my ass to the curb if I fuck up. I'm one thousand percent cool with that, by the way."

"You're so lucky to have them," he wistfully said, tugging at my heartstrings with the pain of his loss. "Being here tonight reminded me of how it used to be with Mom, albeit with more chaos than I'm used to."

I wanted to keep his mood light, so I joked, "Oh, we've got the market cornered on zaniness."

"It's interesting, because being together made me miss Mom so much, but it also was fun and healing to experience that joyous kind of familial love without her. I still wish she was here so she could make Woof costumes and become best friends with your mom. She'd dote on West as the daughter she never had but always wanted. They would've had our wedding planned before dessert the first time they met."

Based on everything I knew about Genevieve, I didn't doubt it. I was sad for all of us that it would never happen. "Not to scare you, but West was already talking about that."

"About us getting married?"

"Yeah."

I worried I had overstepped when he didn't immediately reply, but his response stunned me. "That doesn't scare me."

"It doesn't?"

"Our whirlwind relationship seems very on brand for your family. It would be stranger if they *weren't* already talking about us getting married so soon."

I had to laugh at that. "Oh, you have no idea. We could elope tonight and we still wouldn't be the fastest marriage in the family."

"But we've only been dating since our second meeting on Friday night! It's Sunday; that's not even three full days."

"Mom and Dad got hitched on their first date."

He laughed so hard that tears came to his eyes. "Why am I surprised at this point? Nobody does anything normal in your family. How long did they know each other before that?"

"They met the first day of a creative writing class in college on a Tuesday but didn't talk to each other. They workshopped Mom's story for the next class on

Thursday. Dad approached her after class to tell her how much he loved her writing and wondered if they could go out sometime and get to know each other. Mom asked if he was free then, and he said yes. They had lunch at a restaurant by the courthouse and fell in love hard and fast while talking to each other. After they finished, they went next door and got married, because they were so certain they had found their soul mate in each other." I grinned at Elias's shocked expression.

"Isn't your dad supposed to be the levelheaded one?"

"He's a scientist with a creative side, who is a romantic at heart and thought Mom was magical. To him, marrying her was the most logical decision in the world. His family lost their shit when he told them he had eloped on a whim during a first date with someone he had only spoken to that same day. But Mom being Mom, she charmed them, even though they were all ready to hate her and force them to get an annulment. Nobody expected they'd last, but they've been happily married almost twenty-eight years now."

The amazement on Elias's face was adorable. "Wow, what an incredible story."

"Of course, the irony is I spent so many years making fun of them for rushing into a relationship, and then I basically did the same thing with you. But just like them, the only thing I regret is not meeting you sooner."

He leaned over and kissed me again, reminding me that falling in love with him was the best decision I had ever made.

ONCE WE REACHED Elias's apartment, I walked him to his door. "Thanks for coming over tonight. I'm glad we didn't scare you off."

"I had fun with everyone. It also made me wonder if maybe…"

"Wonder what?"

He took a deep breath before looking at me with endearing shyness. "I wondered if maybe you'd like to come over to my dad's place for dinner next Friday? It won't be nearly as exciting as tonight, but Dad's an excellent cook. You could stay here again if you wanted, spend all day Saturday together, and we could go over to your Mom's on Sunday."

I wrapped my arms around his waist and pulled him into a hug. "I think that sounds like a perfect weekend. Count me in."

His happy smile poured warm sunshine into my soul. "Really?"

"Really. Hell, I'd love to stay here the entire week, but if I do, you'll miss work. I have a few things I need to take care of, so I'm very mad real life wants to ruin our fun."

My heart sang when he looked a little sad that I wouldn't be staying over tonight, even as I hated having to spend time apart from him. However, I wasn't joking about keeping him up all night if I stayed. I also had to get my horoscopes for the week turned in before the deadline.

He sighed in disappointment. "I have an important meeting I can't miss tomorrow, so it's for the best."

"Please know it's taking every ounce of willpower I have to not stay." I hugged him closer. "I'll make it up to you next weekend, promise."

"I'm looking forward to it." He nuzzled against me as he soaked up all the contentment he could from being together before we had to part. "Thanks for making this one of the best birthday weekends I've ever had. I was convinced it would be the worst, but you seem to have an uncanny knack for turning the impossible into reality. I'm so grateful to you and your family for everything you've done for me."

"If I've made you feel even a fraction of how good you've made me feel this weekend, I'm thrilled."

Elias gave me a sweet kiss, which I savored for as long as I could before I forced myself to put distance between us. "If I don't make myself leave now, I'm going to lose my will to do it."

"I know what you mean."

"Good night, Elias. I'll text you when I get home."

I didn't expect him to be so relieved from my promise. "Thanks, I appreciate that. I'm always nervous when people are on the road late."

"Between my mom and sister, I'm very used to checking in, so you never have to worry about that. I'll see you soon."

"Night."

I couldn't resist stealing one last hug and kiss before he went into his apartment with a wave. With the biggest smile on my face, I left full of love and happiness, eager for next Friday to come so we could be together again.

AS I PROMISED, I texted Elias, Mom, and West once I was back at my apartment to let them know I had gotten home without incident.

Felix was sitting on the sofa chair with his laptop in front of the TV, his legs stretched out on the ottoman. He paused the video when he saw me approaching. "Well, well. Look who it is."

Grabbing water from the fridge, I returned to the living room to drop onto the couch. "Hey, man. How's it going?"

"From the looks of it, my weekend wasn't nearly as good as yours."

"You mean you didn't take advantage of having wild kitchen sex while I was gone?"

He scoffed at that. "Please, at this point, I'll take boring sex anywhere. I haven't gotten laid since Danny and I broke up in March. It's not fair when he's out there fucking any guy who has a pulse and no taste."

"As hot as you are, all you need to do is hit a frat house party when school starts next month. You'll have more offers than you can handle."

Felix scowled. "I want to get laid, but I don't want meaningless sex. I prefer actual relationships, which apparently no one our age wants. Every guy who has seemed into me bolts as soon as I bring up commitment. Maybe I need to try dating older guys?"

"If you had asked me Friday morning, I would've said relationships are for chumps. Now, I'd walk down the aisle tomorrow and be happy for the rest of eternity."

I couldn't blame Felix for looking stunned, considering I was notorious for only being interested in no-strings-attached fucks. "Whoa, what the fuck kind of weekend did you have?"

"The best one of my life. Every second I spend with Elias makes me selfishly want a trillion more with him. It was hell pulling myself away from him to come home tonight, when all I wanted to do was curl up in bed with him."

Felix arched an eyebrow at me. "*Just* curl up in bed with him?"

"Yeah, how weird is that?"

"For you? *Really* fucking weird. Next thing you'll be telling me you didn't fuck him." Felix's jaw dropped when I gave him a sheepish shrug. "Holy shit, you spent two nights with a guy and didn't fuck him? *You*? I didn't know that was humanly possible."

I ran my hand through my hair with a sigh. "And I'm completely fine with that, which confuses the shit out of me. A single kiss from him is enough to send me over the moon and back."

"Damn, you fell in love for real, didn't you?"

There was no denying it. "I did, and I'm not scared. What does that mean?"

"You finally grew up," Felix answered with a laugh. "Good for you. I never thought I'd live to see the day where you fell in love, let alone before me."

"Sorry you're going to miss out on your chance to hook up with me." Felix snickered at my joke, although part of me was disappointed I'd never get to enjoy him. But I wanted Elias so much that Felix wasn't an option anymore. How weird was that? "Look at it this way: if you had fallen in love, your Paris trip in two weeks would be a total waste. Just think of all those hot Frenchmen you wouldn't be able to fuck if you had a boyfriend."

Felix ruefully shook his head. "You say that, but knowing my luck, they'll all hate Americans so much that they won't have anything to do with me and my shitty high school French."

"What about Izzy's older brother, Arsène? Isn't he supposed to play tour guide for you?"

He closed his laptop and set it on the coffee table with a dejected huff. "He's only doing that to humor Izzy. A famous thirty-seven-year-old photographer who works with models like Rune won't have any reason to look at a twenty-two-year-old nobody like me twice, let alone lust after me. I'm cute, but I'm not *that* cute."

"Oh, you definitely are. But if that doesn't tempt him, game the system. Make him think he's lost you. He'll keep double-checking you're still with him, which gets him to look at you more."

"And will make him think I'm an incompetent and stupid American kid." Felix curled his legs under him. "Besides, he's so hot that he's *way* out of my league. He'll never see me as anything more than his younger brother's friend."

"His younger brother's *sexy* friend," I corrected. "Trust me, that's a *very* popular romance trope. You'll do great."

Felix rolled his eyes. "There's one problem: this is real life, not a romance novel. It's like the cute boy next door. In my experience, they either don't exist, or if they do, they're straight, an asshole, ugly, or taken. Hollywood lied to us."

"If an unrepentant flirt like me can fall for a cute,

shy sweetheart, you should have no problem getting a hot French guy to fall for you."

Ever the realist, Felix pointed out, "Even if that *were* true, I'd be signing up for a shitty long-distance relationship. I couldn't even make a living-together relationship work without the asshole cheating on me. How would I keep him faithful with an entire ocean between us? Not to mention the temptation of all those gorgeous models he photographs."

"If the only way I could stay with Elias would be to move to France, I'd be on the next plane practicing my French." I never imagined I'd feel that way about a guy, but damn if it wasn't true. "Wow, I have it bad for him, don't I?"

"I'd say," Felix agreed with a chuckle. "Maybe I'll try taking a page out of your book. Why shouldn't I have some fun while I'm on vacation, you know? Now that you've discovered relationships are amazing, it might be time for me to loosen up and learn they aren't the end-all be-all like I have them built up."

"Nothing like trading places to gain some perspective, am I right?"

Felix grinned at me. "Something like that. I don't think I'll ever understand how your world works, though. You live in a totally different realm than the rest of us, where weird, unbelievable shit happening is an everyday occurrence."

Remembering I had water, I took a sip before

putting the cap back on. "Even I wouldn't have believed I'd fall in love this hard so fast."

"I don't know why you're surprised when you're the guy whose parents eloped on their first date. You and Elias spent your first weekend together as a couple and you're not already married or fucking? That's glacial pacing in comparison."

"Well, I guess now it's up to West to announce she married some rando on the day she meets them. That's about the only way to outdo my parents' record."

Felix snorted at that since he had become close friends with my sister during her many hangouts at our place. "I wouldn't put it past her. She's as nuts as you."

"There's no helping it. We are twins, after all." I got up and stretched. "Sorry to cut it short, but I need to get my work turned in to my boss. Talk to you in the afternoon?" I never said the morning because both of us were late sleepers.

"Sounds good." Felix stopped me as I passed him. "North, for what it's worth, I'm super happy for you and Elias. He seems like a great guy. Before I leave, we should have him come over here and hang out with Callum and the rest of the guys."

"And just when I thought my night couldn't get any better." I had always kept my hookups out of the apartment, so having Felix extend an invitation to my boyfriend meant a lot to me. "Thanks, man. I really appreciate that. We'll definitely make that happen."

"I'll try to keep my teasing about you two canoodling to a minimum."

We both laughed as I headed to my bedroom to work on the horoscopes for the upcoming week. It was going to be so much fun planning out the ones for Virgo and Aries to coincide with our plans. I couldn't wait to see how excited Elias would get when they came true.

Chapter Thirteen

ELIAS

IT SURPRISED me how disappointed I was North couldn't spend the night with me after the amazing dinner we had at his Mom's place. While it was the responsible decision, I had enjoyed cuddling with him and having fun exploring each other's bodies. Instead of my normal fear, I fluttered with excitement about the possibility of going all the way with him. It was a mistake to get my hopes up about it being an enjoyable experience. But he had repeatedly proven that if anyone could make the impossible happen, it was him.

Heading into my bedroom, I pulled out the box of cards Mom had written me while she was sick. She had a card for every occasion, all broken into sections and labeled with tabs in her neat handwriting. As I sat on my bed, I couldn't settle on which emotion to feel as I looked at the envelope that said, "When you meet someone special." It didn't get more special than North, that was for sure.

Taking a deep breath, I steadied my nerves as I removed the card my mom illustrated for me. On the front was a simple sketch of two lovebirds nestled together to form a heart against a blue gradient background. There were a few flowers and hearts as a perfect touch. It was such a sweet picture; I was eager to share it with North.

I studied it a few moments longer, appreciating all the little details of her artistry. It bummed me out that of all the wonderful traits I had inherited from her, art hadn't been one of them.

When I was ready, I opened the card. It startled me when a smaller pink envelope fell out addressed, "To the lucky man who loves my son." I set it aside to deal with later before diving into my mom's message to me.

Bertie,

Can you sense how giddy I am that you've found someone special? Didn't your mom do an amazing job of finding you the most surprising Mr. Right ever? You must have been very confused at first, because he's nothing like you imagined you'd end up with (sorry, no stuffy lawyers for you!), but that's half the fun.

I laughed, because she was absolutely correct. Josh had been a stuffy attorney and a disastrous relationship. I used to picture myself being with a calm, older gentleman, so North was the complete antithesis in every way. Despite that, I had never been happier.

With a smile, I continued reading.

You're probably asking yourself, why does this man seem to understand you like nobody else does? Why does he make you forget about being sad and remind you of how much fun it is to live? How is it possible he has the second best mother in the world after me?

I'll give you a hint about the last question: life is too long to spend that many Christmases with a mother-in-law who hates you and thinks you'll never be good enough for her son. I'd rather go to Hell than let you get stuck with that nightmare scenario. If I have my way, you'll have one who is more mom and less in-law. She'll love you twice as much because I'm not there to do it in-person anymore, and someday, you'll feel comfortable enough to call her just Mom (that's a good thing, sweetie! Don't feel guilty, you hear me?). Luckily, I should have enough karma points saved up to cash in, because it's a hell of a big ask from the cosmic universe. But you deserve it, and I was extra nice, so it'll balance out in the end. You'll see.

Anyway, I promise Mr. Right comes with the perfect family who will remind you how to laugh and love without feeling guilty about enjoying yourself when I'm not there. Because if he didn't, he'd be Mr. Wrong and you should RUN.

Once again, I stared at her words with a confused wonder. Was it absurd to feel like Mom had managed the impossible and found me the perfect unexpected boyfriend with the best family ever? But given North's track record with the uncanny, was it such a leap to believe that if anyone could manage that, it'd be him? Didn't it say something important that I could show him her card and he wouldn't assume I had lost my mind for wondering if maybe she had more karmic pull than I imagined was possible?

I kept reading to see if there were more answers in the rest of her note.

Despite being Mr. Right, you're probably questioning if you're moving too fast or making a mistake by wanting to be with someone while you're still in the grieving process. There's nothing wrong with fast, because when you know, you know. If he's truly the one for you, him and his entire family will help you through your grief. I'm sorry if it might have taken me a little longer to get into a position to pull some strings than I'd like. It's hard to make ooky spooky happen quickly! But I've always said people come into our lives at the right time for a reason. That's as true for Mr. Right as it is for anyone.

The best advice I can give you at this point is: believe. Believe your sadness won't last forever. Believe you deserve a loving relationship. Believe the man who sees you for you is the one, even if on paper, he seems like the least likely candidate for a boyfriend ever. Believe your mother loves you and will do absolutely everything in her powers to ensure you live a long and happy life with the man who'll dedicate his life to making you feel loved. More than anything, believe in love and the impossible. Anything is possible when you're in love, right? Even the most impossible things you can imagine.

I leaned back against my bed and reread that paragraph again. How could Mom be *that* accurate? When I saw her next sentence, I laughed.

Creeped out yet?
"Why, yes, Mom, since you mention it, this IS eerily accurate. However did you manage to do that?"
One, I'm awesome. Two, I know you, my dear boy. It's great to curl up with the latest Arrietty Quenby book and read it by yourself. But isn't it so much better to have someone to laugh with about how witty she is afterward? Mr. Right will LOVE her if I have anything to do with it.

An incredulous giggle bubbled up from inside me. "Now you're just messing with me, Mom. You seriously found the one man who loves Arrietty because *she's his mom?* How is that possible?"

It was so unbelievable, I desperately wanted to it to be true. North would get a huge kick out of it when I showed him the note later.

> I'm running out of room, so I'll save my cryptic predictive powers for your next note. Remember, I'll always love you forever, and so will Mr. Right. I'm so proud you listened to my birthday card and showed your clockwork to the man who was meant for you. I told you North would watch over you, love you, and protect you, because that's why he was created. Keep following your heart to happiness, sweetheart.
>
> Enjoying laughing at your shock with all my love,
> Mom

It took me a solid minute to remember she was referring to the bird North she made for my birthday and not my boyfriend who equally fit that description. Glancing around my room, I half expected to see a spectral version of my mother grinning at me. I almost swore I could feel her hugging me, but it didn't make me cry this time. I held on to that warm feeling, as unbelievable as it was to me.

"Well done, Mom. You've outdone yourself, even by your standards. Thank you."

I swore I could hear her laughing in delight.

AFTER OUR MEETING ended the next morning, Rhys requested, "Hey, Elias, do you have a second?" Wearing a well-tailored black suit with a lavender shirt, he was handsome with chiseled cheekbones, a strong jaw, and striking gray-blue eyes. Beyond that, he was a kind person and an incredible boss who treated board members and the janitor with the same level of respect. I admired him for being so nice and making everyone feel like his best friend without trying.

I finished packing up my things to give him my full attention. "Absolutely."

"You did an outstanding job today. We would have lost that deal without your excellent work."

Rhys was a big believer in praise, but it still touched me he would say it when he didn't have to. "Oh, thank you. I'm glad I could help! I worried about getting Terrington to agree to everything, but we worked it out just in the nick of time."

"Thank god, because it would have been a disaster if you hadn't been able to get him to come around." Rhys pushed his chair in and gestured for me to follow him. "How are you doing?"

It was nice I didn't have to lie to answer that question anymore. "Really well, actually. Thanks for asking."

"You seem much happier these days. I'm glad things are getting better for you."

I appreciated he said it with no trace of judgment in his tone. If he had been any other boss, I would have been paranoid that my misery was too apparent. He wasn't that kind of man, thankfully. "They really have been. It's been nice to have reasons to enjoy having fun again."

"I'm so glad to hear that, Elias." We paused outside of my office. "If I can ever do anything to help, let me know."

I appreciated it wasn't an empty offer. Rhys had sent flowers to my mom in the hospital and made sure Dad and I took bereavement leave after she passed away. He and his husband, Lucien, had even come to her funeral, which had stunned me. It was above and beyond what I expected from work. I had been too numb to process it back then, but afterward, their show of support touched me. "Thank you, Rhys."

"Anytime," he said with a warm smile before continuing to his office.

Entering mine, I had barely sat down before Callum appeared with bubbling excitement. His blue suit was paired with a yellow button-down shirt and a hot pink bow tie. He shut my door before taking a seat in front of my desk. "Tell me everything!"

"About what?"

"It was so obvious on Saturday that something's going on between you and North." He was practically bouncing in his chair with giddiness. "I'm dying to find out if I'm right. Please tell me I am."

I tilted my head as I regarded him. "Are you that excited for me to date your friend?"

"Yes, because it would be the best thing ever!"

His enthusiastic reaction made me chuckle. "Why?"

"Because you're perfect for each other."

"Even though we're total opposites?"

Callum scoffed at my protest. "If you're like me and Rune, you'll discover you aren't nearly as opposite as you seem at first."

I suspected there was some truth in his words. "To answer your question, yes, we're boyfriends now."

His delighted squeal was adorable. "How exciting! I'm so happy for you both."

"You weren't kidding about him being unusually perceptive. He understood things about me I never expected."

Callum nodded in agreement. "There's more to him than there first appears. For someone who seems so comfortable with who he is, he has a surprising tendency to underestimate himself. Rune was the same way."

Talk about surprises. How could anyone who as good-looking, smart, and talented as Rune be insecure about anything? "Really?"

"It shocked me, too. I figured he had never spent a single second doubting himself, but it turned out he wasn't used to people accepting certain things about him, so he struggled to take those same parts of himself seriously. It sounds silly, but it helped me realize he was human and not just a gorgeous, perfect god who had descended from Heaven. After I realized that, it was possible for us to grow closer together."

His example made me wonder about North's writing again. Was his tendency to dismiss his work as meaningless erotica because he felt he'd never be able to measure up to his mom's popularity? Was that why he limited fantasy to only his art? "You might be onto something there."

"I'm so happy you found each other," he gushed. I appreciated someone else was as excited as I felt about my situation.

"Thank you for encouraging me to go for it. I'm not sure if I would've been brave enough otherwise."

Callum smiled at me as he reassured me, "I bet you would have surprised yourself. There aren't many who can resist the alluring pull of North's special brand of muchness."

"I don't think I could, even if I wanted to."

His giggle was as cute as him. "That was how I felt about Rune, and we all know that worked out for the best. I'm confident it will with you and North, too."

"Thanks."

"Anyway, I should probably let you get back to work. We'll chat soon?"

"Of course."

With a few more parting words and well-wishes, Callum left with a wave and a happy bounce in his step. I was unaccustomed to people being so genuinely excited for me who weren't Mom. It was… nice. Really nice, actually. Hopefully Dad would be, too.

Getting up to go talk to him before I lost the nerve, I went to his office and knocked on his open door. "Hey, got a minute?"

He looked up at me and smiled, the stress melting away from his face. "For you, always. Come in."

I shut the door behind me and sat down in the chair in front of his cherrywood desk with a spectacular view of the city. The rat Mom had made him out of CDs, Arlo, sat next to his computer monitors, glinting in the sunlight. "How's your day been?"

"It could be better, but I'm glad you're here. What did you want to talk about?"

I rubbed the back of my hand. "It's actually about something personal, not work."

He grew concerned. "Is everything okay?"

"Great, actually. That's sort of what I need to talk to you about."

"You've lost me."

In my nervousness, I blurted out my news. "I have a boyfriend."

My dad's eyes went wide in surprise. "Really?"

"I would have told you sooner, but it's a recent development."

"How recent is 'recent'?"

My pulse raced as I admitted, "This weekend."

"Oh. That's indeed rather…sudden."

I wasn't certain what his reaction meant, which caused my anxiety to spike. "It is, but I'm happy, Dad. For the first time since we lost Mom, I'm really, truly, genuinely happy because of him." Worried about how he might react, I babbled. "He's nice, and funny, and helped me remember how to have fun, and I swear he's nothing like Josh, and—"

Dad held up his hand to stop my rush of anxious words. I bit my lower lip as I waited on pins and needles for him to say something. His voice was calm as he said, "Breathe, Elias."

I drew a shaky breath, still fearful of his reaction. He had insisted the reason he didn't support me being with Josh was because he made me miserable, rather than being uncomfortable with my sexuality. But part of me worried maybe he would never approve of my boyfriends.

He held my gaze as he warmly said, "I'm happy you've met someone who makes you feel that way.

That's all I've ever wanted for you. If he's nothing like that deadbeat Josh, I like him already."

A relieved sigh escaped me. "He's amazing, Dad. His stories are the best, even when they seem almost too unbelievable to be true. And he's so kind and understanding. He's Callum's friend, which is how I met him. I really, *really* like him, and I—I want…" Taking another breath, I forced myself to be brave. "I want to bring him to dinner Friday so you could meet him."

If my dad had looked surprised before, he was downright shocked by my request. "It's that serious even though it's such a new relationship?"

"I rushed into being with Josh, but that was different. While North and I haven't known each other that long, he—"

"North?"

Once again, I couldn't gauge my dad's reaction. "Do you know him?"

"Did you meet him before your birthday?"

Now I was confused. "Yeah, exactly one week before to the day. I was waiting to meet Callum after work on Friday when North came in. The bartender was trying to set us up together. Funny story, it was because of our horoscopes on the website Mom used to read kind of foretold that would happen. But North was also Callum's friend, so he joined us for dinner. One thing led to another, and—"

"Are you telling me your horoscope predicted your new boyfriend, who coincidentally is named North?"

Dad was a man of logic and facts, so he thought horoscopes were a load of nonsense. He had humored Mom's interests and never derided her for believing in them but maintained a healthy dose of skepticism. "It sounds nuts, but—"

I quit talking when he laughed harder than I had heard in a long time. When he regained his composure, he shook his head in disbelief. "Your mother is something else, you know that?"

"What do you mean?"

He leaned back in his black leather chair with a wry grin. "She swore up and down she'd make a believer out of me someday. Leave it to your mom to refuse to give up even in death. She always had to be right no matter what, and she could never resist showing off."

"That's true, but I still don't understand."

"Having you meet a guy named after your birthday present a week before you receive it because a horoscope from her favorite site predicted it has Genevieve's ghostly fingerprints all over it."

It was such a relief he sounded entertained by the idea instead of scandalized. "Oh, it gets weirder. She promised me in one of her notes she'd find me a partner who loved Arrietty Quenby. North's mom *is* Arrietty Quenby, so of course he loves her."

Dad pressed his hand to his forehead as he

snorted in bemusement. "God, your mother never half-asses anything, does she?"

"No, she was a firm believer in whole-assing everything and then some, as she would say." It was a sentiment she had often expressed. "You really don't think I'm foolish for wishing all these coincidences happened because of her influence? It realistically shouldn't be possible, but she's so accurate it makes me wonder."

"If it was anyone but your mother, I'd refuse to believe it and say you were seeing things through the lens of your grief. But I learned long ago not to bet against her. It's so 'ooky spooky' I can hear her giggling with glee about it." A wistful expression flitted over my father's face, reminding me I wasn't the only one who missed her. "I'd enjoy meeting your North if he wants to join us for dinner this Friday. Do you think he'd like my sweet potato chili?"

My heart swelled at the fact Dad wanted to make my boyfriend the dish that had made my mom fall in love with him when they were dating. "I'm sure he will. Thank you for letting me bring him over."

"I'm thrilled you want to introduce him to me."

"Despite it being fast?"

He smiled at my question. "You're talking to the man who fell in love with your mother the first time I heard her giggle before I knew her name. I have no room to talk on that front."

"Thanks, Dad." His reassurance set me at ease. "Want to grab lunch together today?"

He brightened further. "Sure. Let me send two quick emails and we can go if that's okay?"

"Sounds good to me." I heaved a sigh of relief that the conversation had gone better than I had expected. It meant the world to me he was trying so hard to be an active part of my life. Mom would have been so proud of us for learning how to be close. I said a silent thank-you to her for everything.

"Ready?"

I stood up with a nod. "Yeah, let's go."

He came around the corner of his desk and surprised me with a hug. "I'm happy for you, son. Truly."

I held on to him tighter. "Thanks, Dad."

He patted my back before releasing me. "How does Thai sound?"

"Perfect!"

"Fantastic. You can tell me all about North over lunch if you want to."

"I'd like that." With a lightness in my spirit and step, I followed him to our favorite restaurant.

AFTER GETTING BACK from a great lunch with Dad, I still had some time left before I needed to work. I was brimming with curiosity about North's writing, but I felt weird and invasive for asking about something so personal. Then again, Callum had read his work, so he was clearly open to sharing it.

My horoscope that morning had encouraged me to be more willing to ask questions to help me grow closer to the ones I cared about. Was it ridiculous to act on it? Probably. But it was also useful general advice, so what was the harm in doing as it suggested?

I glanced over at the small bird statue on my desk Mom had made for me. "What do you think, Avery? Should I text him?" Silence was my only response, but the answer was obvious. "Yeah, you're right. I should."

Decision made, I typed a quick message to North before I could chicken out and change my mind.

> Would you let me read something you've written?

NORTH

If you wanted to. You're not obligated to, though.

It was an interesting glimpse at his insecurity that I was positive related to who his mom was.

> I genuinely want to read your work.

NORTH

It'll make you blush.

> I'm okay with that.

> My pen name is Finch Northish. If you end up not reading or not liking it, I won't be offended.

I had to shake my head that his pen name was bird-based, given they were my favorite animal.

> Why Finch?

NORTH
> Because if I was an animal, I'd be a Gouldian finch, which are colorful and known for their remarkable head.

I could almost hear him snickering at his own innuendo. However, my curiosity grew about the specific finch he named himself after. A quick search pulled up a cute bird with a yellow body, a purple breast, a green back, with red, yellow, or black faces. It was a spectacularly flamboyant bird and indeed known for their heads of many colors.

> Mom used to sketch those a lot, but I never knew they were real. It's a very fitting name for you. I look forward to getting to know Finch more.

North sent me a flirty emoji, making me laugh. I couldn't wait to see what kind of stuff he wrote, but I had a few more hours at the office to get through first.

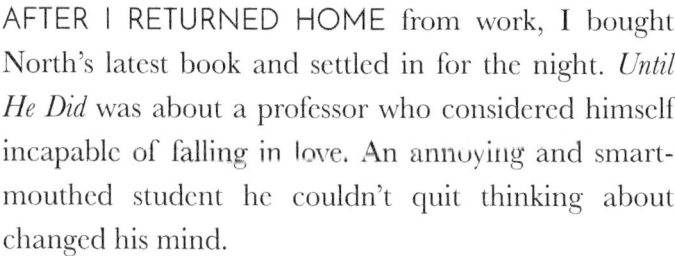

AFTER I RETURNED HOME from work, I bought North's latest book and settled in for the night. *Until He Did* was about a professor who considered himself incapable of falling in love. An annoying and smart-mouthed student he couldn't quit thinking about changed his mind.

As North had promised, it was full of explicit sex scenes that got me hot under the collar. Beyond that, the emotional connection between the two characters struggling with a taboo relationship was incredibly real. Bruce and Jaxon's story was so engrossing that they were more like actual people than characters. I couldn't put the book down until I finished it.

There were touches of Arrietty Quenby's craft in his writing, but it was only because I was aware of their connection; I never would've noticed it otherwise. North's voice was uniquely his own, filling the story with moments that had me laughing out loud. When all I had expected was smut based on his description, it came as a pleasant surprise it was a touching romance.

I checked the watch Dad gave me for my birthday and saw it was almost ten already. Part of me wished I could call North and have him come over to talk about his writing. The mature thing to do would be to wait until Friday to discuss it with him after our dinner with Dad. But I selfishly wished to invite him over, despite being late on a Monday night when I had work the next day.

Remembering my horoscope saying I should learn more about people I cared about by asking questions, now was a fantastic opportunity to do that. Leaving it up to fate, I messaged North.

> It's kind of late, but do you want to come over?

Once again, North was quick to respond. I appreciated it since Josh would rarely answer me, let alone in a timely fashion.

NORTH
For a booty call?

I snorted at the idea I would ever be crass enough for such a thing.

> No, to talk. I read your latest book.

NORTH
Oh god, you hated it, didn't you?

It was strange seeing someone so confident assume the worst about my opinion. The contradictions only made him more intriguing to me. It also was reassuring that he understood me, given I tended to be insecure and anxious.

> I didn't hate it, but I would like to talk about it. If tonight's not great, then maybe Friday night after dinner?

NORTH

I'll be there in sixteen minutes.

His specificity made me note the time out of curiosity.

> Okay, see you soon. Drive safe.

NORTH

I save all my dumbassery for when I'm not behind the wheel, no worries.

Not wanting to distract him from driving, I didn't send a final response letting him know how amusing his answer was.

With him on the way, I wondered whether I should change. My teal plaid pajama pants and purple T-shirt weren't exactly sexy. That unexpected thought brought a blush to my cheeks. Since when had I ever cared about being *sexy*? It was utterly preposterous.

Getting dressed in something nicer was too suspicious, so I stuck with what I was wearing. I killed time browsing on my phone until I heard his knock sixteen minutes later. It sent my butterflies into a tizzy knowing he was on the other side.

Chapter Fourteen

NORTH

WHEN ELIAS OPENED the door wearing his cute pajamas, I wished he had invited me over to do more than talk. There was a hint of desire in his eyes as he drank in the sight of me in a tight black T-shirt and faded jeans. My ego purred, but I reminded it that wasn't why I was there.

He stepped aside to let me in, then offered, "Do you want something to drink?"

"Nope, just your unfiltered criticism." I dropped onto his sofa and kicked off my shoes to make myself comfortable. "I can take it."

Elias sat down next to me with a curious expression. "Why are you so convinced that I have nothing but complaints about your writing?"

"I get that what I write isn't everyone's cup of tea," I said with a shrug.

"For your information, I enjoyed *Until He Did*. A lot, actually."

My eyebrows arched up in shock. "You did?"

"Why does that surprise you?"

There were many reasons, so I started with the most obvious. "You're easily embarrassed, for starters."

"True. I doubt I'd be able to read it out in public, but in private, I really liked it. You have a wonderful writing style, your humor kept me laughing the entire time, and I thought you did a spectacular job at making Bruce and Jaxon feel real. Their emotional and intellectual connection added a fascinating dynamic to the taboo tension. Your book was amazing, North. Please believe I sincerely mean it."

His words touched me, especially since I had braced for the worst. "Thank you for saying that. It means a lot coming from you."

He then asked me an unexpected question. "When your characters have such a rich relationship, why do you keep dismissing it as smut?"

"Because fucking is what I'm known for."

"Yes, but it's not sex for the sake of word count. Watching their emotional bond manifest physically was moving. It was beautiful, especially as someone —" He cut himself off in embarrassment, before awkwardly continuing. "Um, as someone who, uh, was rooting for them to have their happy ending."

His statement came out as more of an uncertain question. "That's not what you meant, is it?"

"It's still true."

"What were you originally going to say?"

Even when he was flustered, Elias was adorable. He tried to wave away the issue. "Something embarrassing. Forget it, it's not important. Your book—"

"Please tell me."

His voice was barely louder than a whisper as he said, "It's too humiliating."

Based on what I knew about his previous history, it wasn't hard to put together the pieces of that puzzle. I was careful to keep all trace of judgment out of my tone. "Let me guess: you were going to say, 'Especially as someone who hasn't experienced that before,' right?"

He stared down at his hands in shame. "Yeah."

I crooked my finger under his chin to force him to meet my gaze when he tried to look away. "Can I let you in on a little secret?"

"Sure."

"I've never experienced that, either."

Elias blinked in confusion. "What do you mean?"

"That kind of love that Bruce and Jaxon have for each other? I've never had that with anyone." I smiled at his baffled expression. "If I followed the advice to write what you know, my books wouldn't be worth reading."

"I don't understand. It was so authentic. How

could you not have had an amazing boyfriend like that before?"

That was a simple answer. "Because I never did the boyfriend thing before you. I had no interest when there were so many hot guys out there to have fun with. As a result, the romance side of my writing is more speculative than based in fact." Since he had admitted to something embarrassing, I figured it was only fair that I do the same. "It's why I have such a hard time taking my romance seriously. The fucking part is what I know best. Being in a real, meaningful relationship with someone I love with all my heart? I'm learning what it's like now because of you."

He looked more puzzled than before. "I'm so confused. You were writing relationships you hoped to have?"

"Yeah, it was what I thought I might want someday, if I was lucky enough to find somebody willing to put up with my shit. At the same time, dating a Bruce-type would never work for me, because his position as an authority figure would rub me all wrong." That was a massive understatement. I was too much of a contrarian asshole to take orders from a daddy-type. Sadly, I had learned that one the hard way. "But that's how Bruce wanted to be written, and it worked perfectly for Jaxon, so I ran with it."

"How Bruce wanted to be written? The character has a say in that?"

I grinned at his confusion. "Trust me, I'm fully

aware that I sound batshit insane when I say I write what the characters tell me to. I learned early on that trying to force them to do what I wanted never ended well."

"Huh, how fascinating."

It was a relief he wasn't turned off by my creative process. "Wow, I'm super glad you feel that way and not 'Kindly get your schizophrenic ass the fuck out of my apartment, please.'"

That drew a quiet chuckle from him. "I'm assuming it's something akin to the concept of muses that speak to you, rather than a psychiatric disorder. It's hardly the weirdest thing I've heard from someone who was creative. Mom used to have entire conversations with her art pieces as she made them, and her hot glue gun, Murray. They had a contentious relationship because 'he' always insisted on burning her. She went off on Murray more than she ever fought with Dad."

"Well, who could blame her when it sounds like Murray was such a dick?"

I relished the giggle my joke earned me, but Elias returned to the previous topic. "You really haven't had that kind of relationship with someone before?"

"Look, I'm young, fuckable, and always down for a good time. I've fucked around a lot, because it was fun and felt fantastic. Sometimes I didn't even know the dude's name, because it literally didn't matter. I wasn't looking for relationships; I wanted to get my rocks off with a sexy guy. I'm not ashamed of that. I religiously used protection and got tested, because I'm not a total moron. If you want to check my negative tests, they're on my phone."

"I believe you," he softly said. "I feel like there's a 'but' coming, though."

Ignoring my normal instinct to make a joke about butts and coming, I stayed focused. "That's because there is."

The fear in his gorgeous gray eyes was a hard punch in the gut as he guessed, "But that's because you're not interested in a real relationship?"

I took his hand in mine and gave it a reassuring squeeze. "No, you changed everything for me from the moment I saw you."

"*Oh.*"

"Elias, for the first time in my life, I'm not interested in fucking and forgetting you like everyone else. You're all I can think about. I'm desperate to get to know you, hear how your day was, cuddle you, and not be a meaningless repeat fuck buddy. More than that, my goal is to be a perfect boyfriend. I want to treat you right, give you everything your asshole exes denied you, love you, and make love to you. You're the only person I've ever believed I could have the kind of relationship I write about. I don't care that we haven't been together that long. I love you. I crave you, god, I need you so much it fucking *hurts*, and—"

I made a surprised noise when he pulled me in for

a demanding kiss. It was rare to be dominated, and I let him take everything he wanted from me as his tongue moved against mine, claiming me for his. I slipped my hands under his shirt to caress his back as I held him close. The best part was his pajama pants did a shit job of hiding how aroused he was getting.

When we paused for air, I assumed he'd apologize for his boldness. To my great surprise, he requested with more confidence than I would have expected, "Show me."

"How much I want you?" I removed his shirt after he nodded. I kissed along his neck as I groped his perfect ass. "How much I love you?"

"Please."

Who could say no to that?

We moved to his bedroom, where we rid ourselves of our clothes. After giving me a bottle of lube and condom, he set his glasses on the nightstand.

As soon as Elias got in bed, I pinned him in place under me. I told him with every kiss and touch how wild I was about him and how he was everything I needed in life. He was putty in my hands as I pleasured him to the fullest, working my way down with mounting anticipation. I teased him with a blow job, making sure he was into it before slipping a slicked finger into him while moaning around his length.

His asshole ex-boyfriends had made sex a painful and unenjoyable experience, so I was determined to do everything in my power to change that for him. I moved down to tease his balls as I slid my fingers inside of him. "Is this okay?"

"It doesn't hurt."

Not hurting was a start, but I wouldn't be satisfied until he felt great. I continued lavishing oral attention on his sac as I worked on getting him used to the sensation of spreading him open.

When I was confident he could handle a third, I refocused him by going down on him again. I hummed low in my throat as I took him deep, earning me the most delightful sounds of enjoyment from him. When his muscles tensed around me, I caressed the spot inside him I knew would make him come undone.

He came with a soft cry, and I enjoyed swallowing the evidence of his satisfaction. Still working him with my fingers, I asked, "Feeling good?"

"Incredible, but…um…"

"You can tell me."

"I was hoping—well, I wanted to see if I…" He covered his face with his hands and groaned, before mumbling, "If I could come from you being inside me."

Fuck, if he kept talking like that, I would blow my load before I entered him. "There's no 'could' about it. You will."

He propped himself to look down at me with a quizzical expression, even though I was a blur without his glasses. "But I already did."

"And you will again."

"*Again?*"

Damn those fuckwits for being so cruel to him. "Promise."

"But that's not possible."

"Sure it is."

He scoffed as he fell back onto the bed. "If you say so."

"Are you ready?"

Elias took a shaky breath. "Yeah."

I withdrew my fingers to put on the condom. "If it hurts or you need me to stop, I will. I swear I won't get mad if you change your mind."

"No, I want this," he said with more conviction.

I moved up so he could see me. "You'll probably tighten up instinctively because you're expecting pain. Remember to breathe and be patient with yourself, okay? You have my word; I won't rail you into the mattress. I only want to give you pure bliss."

"Okay."

Lining myself up with his entrance, I eased into him. As I had predicted, he immediately tensed up. It took some time for him to relax as he realized I wouldn't brutishly shove all the way in and pound him like a piston.

"Sorry, I'm good."

With his consent, I continued easing into him. The slow pace was radically different from all the fast and furious horny fucks in my past. I was dedicated to making sure Elias enjoyed himself. My gratification was the last thing on my mind.

After several stops and starts, I was buried to the hilt. He was so tight I had to bite back a swear, not wanting him to misunderstand my cursing over it being incredible and not because I was mad at him. "Doing okay?"

Elias tensed around my length and it took epic willpower not to move into his action. He reached out to me but stopped. It broke my heart when he asked in a small voice, "Am I allowed to touch you? I don't want to be too clingy."

There wasn't a Hell terrible enough for those bastards. Swallowing down my anger, I gently encouraged him, "Hug me, hold me, dig your nails into me, wrap your legs around me, do whatever feels good. Touch me to your heart's content. It's awesome for us both."

After he looped his arms over my neck, I stuck to shallow thrusts at first, not wanting to overwhelm him. He clenched up, so I let my hands rove over his skin to silently assure him he was safe.

Only once he relaxed did I add more vigor into my movements. As I worked up to a satisfying rhythm, I finally wrung out of him the cutest surprised "*Oh!*" I grinned as I repeated my actions, and he laced his fingers through my hair with a gasp that was verging on pleasure.

I canted his hips to hit deeper, and he rewarded

me with the most glorious "Ah, *North!*" I had ever heard.

"That's it," I encouraged him, continuing to caress him as I pushed in deep. "Fuck, you feel so good."

It was hard not to laugh at his amazed, "I do feel good!"

I leaned forward to kiss him, causing him to cry out in lust at the shift in positions. He clutched on to me as if I was everything to him in that moment. It was the most incredible experience of my life watching him discover pleasure during sex. I was more determined than ever to make sure he enjoyed every single second.

Chapter Fifteen
ELIAS

AT BEST, I had hoped for sex with North to be not painful. Anything more than that seemed like an impossible dream. The glimmers of good were unexpected, but once I gave myself over to him, it turned to mind-blowing pleasure. Every thrust of his hips sent me soaring higher. I lost myself in the glorious sensations overwhelming me, becoming vocal for the first time. It was too amazing to be self-conscious about my sighs and gasps when they drove him wild.

I wrapped my legs around his waist on instinct, practically shouting when he took advantage by groping my ass to guide the rhythm and push in deeper. The only thing keeping me anchored was my hold on him, as the rush of emotions and physical sensations overwhelmed me.

That was why it came as a complete shock when he reached between us and stroked my renewed hardness that I hadn't thought was physically possible. The combined pleasure caused me to shout his name, earning me an enthusiastic "Fuck yeah!" in return from him. *Fuck yeah, indeed.*

It was more than I could handle. I tensed as the tingle of a second orgasm swept over me, whimpering a desperate plea for release.

"Shit, I'm so close," North groaned, his hips ceaselessly driving into me. "I love you, Elias. So. Damn. Much!"

I had never been told in the middle of sex that someone loved me. His sincerity pushed me over the edge. I came all over his fist and my stomach, moaning when it triggered his orgasm.

North braced himself on trembling arms, staying close enough for me to see the awe on his face. He looked at me with more adoration than I knew a person could feel. It surpassed what was in his book, something I hadn't known was possible. The words fell out of my mouth as if they were the easiest thing in the world to say. "I love you, too."

As he kissed me, I wondered why they called it falling in love when it felt more like a rush of flying high. Not even the realization that I had spent years blaming myself for Will and Josh's inadequacies when there was never anything wrong with me could bring me down.

He brushed my temple with his clean hand. "How are you feeling?"

It was impossible to pick any one adjective, so I settled for saying, "Indescribably incredible. *Wow*."

"Me, too." He gave me a lingering kiss on the forehead before getting out of bed. "I'll be right back."

The abruptness of his departure abruptly crashed me down to Earth with bone-shattering force. Josh always showered after sex, so having North go straight to the bathroom was a devastating blow. It was all the more traumatizing because it was unexpected from him of all people. Tears welled up in my eyes as my doubts barreled into me at top speed. The crushing pain made it harder to breathe as I struggled in vain to argue against my fear that it was a terrible coincidence.

North returned immediately, sitting next to me and leaning in to allow me to make out his concerned expression. "What's wrong?"

"Josh always got in the shower as soon as he finished, like being with me made him filthy, and I thought—"

He looked horrified. "Shit, no, no, no! That wasn't what I was doing. I'd never do that to you, Elias. Never."

"Then why did you leave?" I asked in a small voice, hating how pathetic I sounded.

"So I could take care of you and then snuggle the hell out of you for the rest of the night."

That hadn't been the answer I had expected at all. "Take care of me?"

North held up a washcloth. "I figured you wouldn't want to cuddle covered in cum, so I was going to wash you off instead of making you get up. That's literally the *only* reason I would leave you after something as awesome as what we just did. Sorry, I thought I was being helpful. I never meant to upset or hurt you. I didn't wait because I was super stoked to hold you."

I hid my face in my hands with a relieved sob, moved by the show of consideration no one had shown me before; that possibility hadn't occurred to me. "I'm so sorry."

"You have nothing to apologize for," North reassured me as he cleaned me. The warm washcloth was further proof of his thoughtfulness. "I should have explained what I was doing instead of leaving without saying anything. That's on me. I'm the dumbass who owes you an apology. I wasn't thinking."

"No, I shouldn't have assumed you would do the same thing as him. It's not fair to you when all you've done is treat me with kindness."

Satisfied I was clean, North tossed the washcloth onto my nightstand, then moved my hands from my face to look at me. "Please don't beat yourself up because of this. That bastard doesn't deserve to steal this happiness from you, too. I promise I'll never do that again."

Nodding, I did my best to not blame myself. "I appreciate that. The being clean part is nice, though."

"Then I'll always do that for you, but I promise to wait before doing it next time, okay?" He wiped my tears as he smiled at me with an affection that eased my sorrow. "Now, do you want me to spoon you, or would you rather curl up on me?"

"Spoon, please."

"You've got it." He kissed me once more before climbing into bed on the other side.

He slid behind me, then pulled me flush against him. His protective embrace was so comforting I almost cried again. Being held after making love was something both of my ex-boyfriends had denied me, so it meant everything to me he wanted to do it. I melted against him with a contented murmur, my upset fading fast as my earlier satisfaction suffused me once more.

"For the record, cuddling you is a very, *very* close second for the best thing in the entire world," he said as he hugged me tight. "First is reaching sexual nirvana by being with you."

I snuggled against him, loving that he allowed me to do that. "I couldn't agree more."

"Sign me up for a lifetime of this forever, please."

His words suffused me with a warm glow of contentment. "Nothing would make me happier."

"A life dedicated to making you happy is a one

worth living." North kissed the back of my shoulder, and I fell for him anew. "Good night, Elias."

"I love you."

He squeezed me tight. "I love you, too. I'll show you how much in the morning."

It delighted me to discover that falling asleep laughing and in love rounded out the top three most extraordinary experiences ever.

WHEN I WOKE UP, I once more found myself curled around North as I used his shoulder for a pillow. Unlike the first time, I didn't have the immediate knee-jerk fear that I had to move away before I got in trouble for being too clingy.

There was a satisfying soreness in my muscles that served as a reminder of what we had done the previous night. I figured North had been all talk, but he had shown me pleasures beyond my wildest dreams. Yet again, he had made the impossible a reality. Would that ever stop being miraculous?

Part of me wanted to call into work sick so I could enjoy more time with him. However, my responsible side reminded me why I couldn't play hooky because of all the important things I had to take care of at the office later. It was disappointing, but I didn't want to dwell on it and ruin my morning cuddle.

When I nuzzled against him, he reflexively draped

his arm over my waist but remained asleep. It filled me with indescribable joy that his unconscious instinct was to hold me closer. In his embrace, it felt as if nothing could harm me. His confidence made me feel invincible, like I could conquer all my dark demons Will and Josh had left with me.

I shivered when his fingers brushed against my skin as he shifted under me. To soothe him, I caressed his shoulder, earning me a sleepy sigh. It drew my attention to the fact that he had pitched another tent in my sheets. I couldn't hold in a snicker at the blurry image. It probably had more to do with him being twenty-two and horny than it did with me, but it was still a nice ego stroke that maybe I had inspired it.

"Thank god I'm egotistical enough not to get a complex about you laughing at my dick," he teased, his voice thick with sleep. The rough sound of it sent a shudder through me.

"Sorry, its punctuality amuses me."

He snorted at my answer. "I'll take being amused over being offended by it."

"Should I do something about—"

"Again, there's no 'should' in this relationship. My dick is not your responsibility."

His statement was too strange to process. "Huh?"

"Remember how I said I was going to show you how much I love you in the morning?"

"Yeah." His reminder of the promise sent a thrill through me.

"This is how."

"You've lost me."

North guided me to look at him. "I want you to understand that we don't have to have sex every time I have an erection. You're allowed to not be in the mood when I am. I won't get mad if I'm turned on at an inconvenient time for you and have to take care of myself."

For such a simple concept, it was difficult to understand what he was saying. "Do you not want me—"

Before I finished my sentence, North emphatically assured me, "Of course I want you. I want you all the goddamn time. But that's the point—I don't get to have you whenever I want. You can tell me no. I *want* you to tell me no when you aren't feeling it. There's going to be a point when I haven't seen you all week, and when we finally meet up, you'll be too exhausted to do anything. That's okay."

Will and Josh had always insisted I give in to their demands for sex whenever they wanted it, so his point was almost beyond my comprehension. "But won't that disappoint you?"

"Snuggling with you is never a disappointment."

When I remained silent in my disbelief as I tried to process my feelings on the matter, North added, "I don't want you to think that just because we've been together means I always expect sex from you. You're probably still sore, plus you have to go to work soon. Lazing around is its own form of pleasure."

It was a concern I hadn't realized was an issue, so his consideration impressed and touched me. "Thank you. That means more than I can tell you." I leaned down for a kiss, loving the way he caressed my hair as he let me take my time exploring his mouth.

We both jumped when my alarm went off, making North laugh as I hit my phone multiple times on the nightstand before I turned it off. I disabled my other alarms while I was at it.

"I'm sorry I can't skip work today to spend the day together. Being responsible sucks."

Instead of huffing and getting angry like my exes would have, he teased me, "If that's the worst downside to dating an older man, I can live with it."

It was strange thinking of myself in that role when sometimes North seemed far older and wiser than me. "If I could, I would."

"I know." He ran his fingers through my hair to soothe my guilt. "Don't worry, we'll have plenty of time to play this weekend."

"I'm definitely looking forward to it." His words set fire to my desire, emboldening me. "I appreciate you respecting my boundaries, but what if I wanted to do something now?" I almost laughed again when his reaction to my question caused my sheets to twitch above his arousal.

"Such as?"

"Um, do you want to maybe join me in the shower?"

"If you're inviting me to get wet and naked with you, I'm all in." I chuckled at his enthusiasm. "I can't promise I'll keep my hands to myself, though. That's too much temptation to resist."

Having the ability to say "no" to him made me want to tell him "yes" even more. "Then don't resist."

North's blue eyes filled with a hunger that sent my heart racing as my cock responded to being the object of his desire. "Lead the way."

As soon as we were in the shower, North embraced me under the spray while kissing me with a passion that left me breathless. His hands roamed over my body, following the path of the water as he touched me everywhere. It stoked my desires, which stripped away my normal inhibitions. I mirrored his actions, amazed at my lack of hesitation as I groped his firm ass to bring him close enough for our erections to brush against each other.

He went one step further by dipping his fingers between my checks to tease my entrance. Knowing what pleasures he could give inspired need rather than fear and disgust. I ached for more than a teasing touch, though.

To encourage him, I reached down to stroke his hardness. He rumbled in approval before he returned the favor. I gripped his shoulder with my free hand as I enjoyed the endless loop of pleasure echoing between us. It got even better when he kissed up my neck.

North moaned my name before he tugged on my earlobe with his lips. It was beyond me why that was so arousing, but it pushed me toward my climax as we continued jerking each other off. I whimpered when he brushed his thumb over the head of my cock, making me weak in the knees. How did he make the simplest things feel better than they ever had before?

When he reached back to tease my hole once more, I came on his stomach with a loud gasp. Combined with the heat of the shower, the intensity was enough to make me light-headed. His next kiss was dizzying as he claimed my mouth for his.

I surrendered to him as I kept working his hard length. Hearing him sigh my name in ecstasy as he climaxed did wonders for my soul.

Uncaring of the mess between us, North hugged me closer. I kissed him, eager for more mornings to start that way.

Chapter Sixteen

NORTH

BEING intimate with Elias made me realize how much I wanted him—no, *needed* him. It wasn't just that I couldn't quit fantasizing about him every time I got myself off when I was alone. It was seeing his smile, holding him close to me, the smell of him, the feel of him. All of it filled me with a longing like I had never experienced before. While we texted throughout the week, I still had a fierce need for him.

The more annoying problem was that much time apart gave me ample space to overthink things. At first, I had thought encouraging Elias through the horoscopes would be harmless fun. But after hearing his excitement about how many of them had come true lately, I wondered if maybe I was doing the wrong thing.

As soon as my sister came over to my apartment Thursday morning, she saw straight through me. West sat down on the couch with a bounce, wearing a black pinstripe overbust corset with interspersed grommets and a bandolier belt across it. It was topped off with two small pocket pouches at the hip. She paired it with tight black britches and the military high-heel boots from last weekend. To make up for the understated monochrome outfit, she wore vibrant rainbow glitter ombre eyeshadow and lipstick, topped off with matching rhinestones under her eyes. "You're too miserable for someone with the cutest boyfriend ever."

Sitting on the sofa seat next to the couch, I sighed with frustration. "I'm so worried I'll fuck this up."

"In fairness, you have a remarkably consistent track record of being a dumbass who says the wrong thing."

I glared at my twin. "Thanks, that *really* helps."

West shrugged. "Hey, facts are facts. Is there something specific you're worried about, or more just general angst that Elias is too good to be true?"

"His mom was a religious reader of horoscopes on the Signs of the Times site I write for."

"And?"

"When she passed away, he continued reading them to be closer to her."

West seemed as if she didn't know whether to coo or be sad. "That's sweet."

"He feels they brought us together, so I ran ones this week to make him happy about them coming true," I explained. "But the more I think about it, I'm lying to him about who I really am. He deserves to know the truth, but I'm so scared that if I tell him, I'll lose him." Especially now that we had been intimate, it would be an even worse breach of trust.

"Isn't it better to confess when you're in the beginning of your relationship instead of him finding out in five years? *That* would be betrayal."

It was true, but things weren't so simple. "If he finds out it's me, it'll shatter his illusion about something important that comforted his mother when she was battling pancreatic cancer. They meant so much to her and mean a lot to him because of that. I don't want to take that away from him."

"Is he a true believer in their power or is it more it was his mom's thing so he's fond of them?"

"I'm pretty sure it's the latter. I can't bear him thinking I'm manipulating him, though."

West took off her boots so she could fold her legs under her. "I mean, you kind of are if you're writing horoscopes specifically for him."

It was exactly what I didn't want to hear. I threw myself against the cushions with a huff. "That's the problem! Both of his exes were horrible liars, so I'm scared he'll see this as a stab in the back and dump me."

"Dating you aside, Elias seems reasonable." I rolled my eyes as West's dig as she continued. "If you're up-front with him and explain yourself, I'm sure he'll at least hear you out. He's not some drunk frat boy who'll fly off the handle over the smallest slight. Once he gets over the initial shock, he'll understand. But you have to tell him."

"I know you're right," I said with another weary sigh. "I'm scared I'm going to lose him over this."

"Not to add pressure, but Mom and I will never forgive you if it does." She was probably only half-joking.

Her words did nothing to lessen the anxious pit in my stomach. "I'm damned if I do, and damned if I don't."

"You'll be more fucked if you don't, so grab your balls, and do the right thing after dinner at his dad's tomorrow." She made it sound so easy. "We'll all look back at this and laugh someday, so there's no reason to draw things out and make it more painful than it needs to be."

"I hope you're right." It looked like I'd be making an important amendment to tomorrow's horoscopes for Virgo and Aries before they went on the site.

"Of course I am! I'm always right." She laughed, but I couldn't quite share her humor. "Speaking of tomorrow, I've made you an incredible outfit for your dinner. You're going to look so good that even if Elias gets mad at you, he won't be able to stay that way for long."

I'd take any help I could get, including overly

fancy clothes. If I was going to make an ass out of myself, I could at least look hot while doing it.

AS WE PULLED up outside of Elias's dad's house Friday night, I had to swallow down my nervousness. "Fuck, I owe you an apology."

Elias put the car in park. He looked so cute in his black suit and rimless glasses. "About what?"

Because my mom and sister were so easy to get along with, I had severely underestimated what Elias went through coming over to the house. "I didn't realize how nerve-racking it is meeting your partner's family. This shit's scary as hell."

"It's definitely intimidating."

"That's an understatement."

"If it helps, you already have bonus points because you're not Josh and you make me happy." Elias leaned over to give me a comforting kiss. "I promise, just be yourself, and you'll be fine."

Getting out of the car, I grabbed my gift for his dad from the trunk. If nothing else, at least I looked fucking amazing. West had made me a blue corset vest with black trim that accentuated all my lines. She had sewn a matching button-down shirt, black tie, and tailored jacket that fit me like a glove.

The bright teal with cotton candy pink trimming

three-story home screamed Genevieve. "Your mom had a flair for everything, didn't she?"

"I'm still amazed that Dad let her do that," Elias said as he looked at the house with a smile.

We walked up the stairs together, but he stopped me before letting us in. "If I didn't mention it before, you're extra handsome tonight. That jacket and vest really bring out the blue in your eyes."

"And the pants make my ass look fucking fabulous."

Elias laughed before giving me another kiss. "They do. Thanks for getting fancy."

"Anything for you." I reminded myself not to get any inappropriate ideas before meeting his father, then promptly ignored myself. "Wait until you see how good it looks on your floor."

He cracked up as he let us into the house. "Dad, we're here!"

The home was as impeccably decorated as Elias's apartment, with touches of art everywhere that I assumed were his mom's work. I hoped I could take a tour later.

A deep male voice called out, "Great! I'm in the kitchen!"

Elias led the way as I snuck glances all around. A gorgeous guitar glittering in the corner caught my eye, with a stunning floral decorative motif of shattered CD mosaic pieces. Genevieve was everywhere in the home, and even though I had never met her, it felt like she was still there through her art.

The kitchen was worthy of a Michelin-star chef's restaurant. But my attention was drawn to Elias's father, who was a handsome preview of what I had to look forward to as we grew older. He wore a rainbow apron over his work clothes as he stirred a large pot, with his suit jacket draped over one of the bar chairs by the island. It was surprisingly colorful for a man I had been told would be soft-spoken and calm. That was when it belatedly occurred to me it was probably Genevieve's. My heart hurt for both of them.

"Hey, Dad. Sorry, we're a little late." Elias hugged his father hello.

"My meeting also ran longer than expected, so don't worry about it. Dinner should be ready in a few more minutes." His father wiped his hands on the bottom of his apron as he turned his attention to me. "Hi, I'm Elijah Forthwright. Nice to meet you, North. Thanks for coming over."

I shook his hand. "It's a pleasure, Mr. Forthwright. I appreciate you having me."

"Please, call me Elijah. Being called Mr. Forthwright makes me feel like I'm at a deposition with a pissed-off opposing counsel."

"I hope it's okay that I brought you something." I held out the tall, red holographic bag to him.

"Oh, you didn't have to do that!" He took the bottle out and his eyebrows raised in surprise.

"Wysandria wine? Wow, you're really trying to impress me, aren't you?"

Wysandria wines were award-winning and known for their high price point, so it was an understandable reaction. "Nah, if I was trying to impress you, I'd tell you that my mom co-owns it."

"She does?"

"Yeah, her best friend always wanted to own a vineyard with a bed-and-breakfast. Mom promised if she got a big enough advance on a book, she'd go in half on the investment to make Sandria's dream come true. The 'Wy' part of the name is from her husband, Wyatt. Although, Sandria jokes it's because Wyatt's favorite thing to ask her is, 'Why, Sandria?' Like Mom, she has a reputation for being over-the-top, so it's a fair question."

Elijah chuckled. "It sounds like the two of them and Genevieve would have had the wildest brunches imaginable."

"From the stories I've heard of her, that's definitely true." It was sad that would never happen.

"Well, consider me impressed," Elijah said as he put the wine in the chilling fridge. "Thank you, North. That was very thoughtful of you."

"Anything I can do to help?"

"We could set the table?" Elias suggested.

Elijah stirred the pot again as he nodded. "That would be great."

Elias showed me where the flatware was as he got

out the bowls we would be using. It featured an elegant and expressive two-toned silver-and-gold engraved abstract pattern. As I helped set the dinner table, I commented, "This silverware is beautiful."

"I almost divorced Genevieve before we were married over that," Elijah said with a laugh. "She rejected two hundred and twenty-nine other flatware patterns before settling on that one when we were making our registry. Naturally, it had to be special ordered from a custom artisan in Portland. At that point, I was so grateful that she had finally picked something, I was willing to pay whatever it cost."

"Mom was notorious for being able to pick the most expensive thing." Elias began pouring drinks. "She always wanted the best of everything."

"Well, that's because she was the best, right?" I asked, hoping I wasn't overstepping.

"She sure was." Elijah cleared his throat as a wistful expression disappeared as quickly as it had appeared. "So, Elias tells me you're also an artist?"

I helped take the drinks to the table. "Yeah, I make sculptures out of stuff I find. When I was growing up, Mom always acquired weird things while researching her books. I'd tinker with it after she finished a project. I seemed to have a knack for it, so she encouraged me to experiment more. My twin, West, is an amazing fashion designer and sketch artist. I keep telling her she could sell her drawings, but she thinks she has to become famous before they're worth anything."

"Wait, does that mean she made the dress I saw her in last weekend?"

"Yeah, she makes all of her own clothing. I'm not joking when I say she has a two-bedroom apartment, where she sleeps in one room and the other is her closet."

He looked more amazed than before. "Even the corset?"

"She got into making those about two years ago, and now it's all she wears."

"Really? But aren't they hard to breathe in?" Elijah asked as he ladled out the chili for dinner.

"Sure, if you tight-lace them to shrink your waistline to like eighteen inches. But when worn normally, they're actually comfortable. Not to mention they do wonders for your posture. You forget you have it on."

Elias shook his head. "How is that possible? Wouldn't you pass out?"

"I'm wearing one now and I haven't keeled over yet."

They gave me matching puzzled looks as he asked, "You are?"

"This is a corset vest West made me."

"Your sister designed that?" Elijah gave an impressed whistle. "Wow, she's quite talented, isn't she?"

"She is, but I don't understand how that's a corset," Elias said in confusion.

I shrugged out of my jacket and turned to show them the cinched binding of the back of the vest. The four lines of curved piping made me look extra fuckable when combined with how nice and tight my ass was in the tight black slacks. I couldn't blame Elias for inhaling sharply at how sexy the view was. Glancing at him over my shoulder with a smirk, I very much enjoyed watching him struggle against his desire.

"If she isn't selling her clothes yet, she definitely should start. That tailoring is impeccable." Elijah continued dishing out our dinner.

"That doesn't hurt at all?" Elias asked as I put my jacket back on.

"If it did, I wouldn't be wearing it." I couldn't resist being myself, so I added, "I can even bend over in it."

Elijah snorted at that as his son turned into a blushing cherry. We carried the bowls over to the table and took our seats.

"This smells amazing. What kind of chili is it?"

"Sweet potato. It's an old family recipe, so I promise it tastes better than it sounds."

At the taste of the first bite, I couldn't hold back my appreciative hum at the rich flavors. "This is delicious! It's got a nice little kick to it, too."

It was cute seeing how much Elias resembled

Elijah in the way they both humbly took compliments. "Thank you. That would be the cayenne."

"This is the dish that made Mom fall in love with Dad."

"Well, I guess it's a good thing I was already in love with you before eating this, otherwise, this might have been a very confusing dinner."

I grinned as my joke got a big laugh out of them both. Elias was right; as long as I was myself, everything would work out.

AFTER WE FINISHED, Elias went to the bathroom. I was grateful for the chance to talk to Elijah in private. "Thanks for letting me come over here tonight."

"I appreciate you giving my son his smile back. It's been a long time since I've seen him be so carefree."

"I genuinely love him."

Elijah smiled at me. "Oh, of that I have no doubt. I can't tell you what it means to me to see you both so happy and in love with each other. I worried Elias would close himself off after losing his mom. You may not have been together very long, but I can tell you've made all the difference in the world to him already."

It was the perfect chance to ask what I hoped wasn't insensitive. "Speaking of her, could I make a request? And if I'm way out of line, please feel free to tell me no."

"Sure."

"Would you be willing to part with a few pieces of Genevieve's silverware? I want to build a bird out of them as a partner to keep Elias's clockwork North company. I wouldn't need much. Maybe three spoons, two forks, and a butter knife?"

I held my breath as I waited for his answer. Thankfully, he didn't get upset. "Genevieve would love that. I'll roll some up in a napkin and slip them in with a dessert for you to take home. Make it with her blessing and mine."

"Thank you, Elijah."

"Thank you for what?" Elias asked as he came back.

Not wanting to lie, I sidestepped with a separate truth. "For having me over and cooking such a delicious dinner."

"Oh, it's been my pleasure. Hopefully, you'll enjoy dessert just as much. I'm making a s'mores casserole. It's all the fun of s'mores with no fire pit required."

"That sounds excellent!"

Elias lit up at the mention of the dish. "You'll love it."

"We can also open that wonderful wine now that it's chilled. Until then, if you want to check out some of Genevieve's work, we have time while it's in the oven."

My night kept getting better and better. "Great! I'd love to hear the story behind that mosaic guitar I saw earlier."

WE RETURNED to Elias's apartment after dinner. It hadn't been as lively as the one at my family's house, but it had been fun. I hadn't seen his father put in the silverware I had requested, but I could feel it in the bag. It was almost as heavy as the weight on my heart over what I needed to do. I hoped like hell I wasn't about to ruin the best thing that had ever happened to me.

After putting the dessert in the fridge, I sat Elias on his sofa. "Can I talk to you?"

"Always."

With a deep breath, I warned myself not to be a coward. "There's something important I haven't been entirely up-front with you about. It's about my writing."

"What about it?"

"You know about my work as Finch Northish, but there's more to my writing career than that."

I didn't blame him for looking confused. "What do you mean?"

"Three years ago, an opportunity to be a part-time writer on a website came up. I thought it would be easy money that would help me pay for self-publishing my novels, so I accepted the position."

"Okay, so what's the problem with that? Is it like a kink blog or something?"

His response normally would've made me laugh, but my fear had too strong of a hold on me. Now was the moment of truth. "No, it's Signs of the Times."

"Oh, because of your aunt?"

"Yeah, I got the job through her after one of their writers abruptly quit and they couldn't find a fast replacement. I write the daily horoscopes."

An incredulous bubble of laughter erupted from Elias. "You're joking, right?"

"Not about this," I said as I held his gaze to convey my seriousness. "Every horoscope you and your mom have read in the last three years have all been written by me."

The humor faded from his countenance. "So all the recent ones that have been so accurate…"

"I swear I wasn't trying to manipulate or lie to you. But I loved seeing how excited you got when they came true, plus I'd liked the idea of being able to give you some anonymous encouragement when things were hard. More than anything, I didn't want to ruin your tradition or your memories of horoscopes with your mom. The more I thought about it, the more I realized that my good intentions might be harmful, so I had to tell you. The one from the day we met was a total coincidence, though. I turn them in a week in advance and had no idea I'd be meeting you that night."

He stared at me with an unreadable expression, causing my fear to skyrocket. An uncomfortable silence hung between us, telling me I had officially fucked up beyond repair. With a heavy heart, I stood up from the couch. "Sorry, I should go."

It stunned me when he tugged on my hand to force me to sit again. His voice was harsher than I was used to as he exclaimed, "No, you don't get to drop that on me and then run away! You're going to stay here, and we're talking this out like adults."

I sat mute, awaiting his judgment.

Chapter Seventeen

ELIAS

"SORRY, THAT CAME OUT WRONG," I apologized. "Please stay so we can talk this out? I didn't mean to snap at you."

North's chastised look tugged at my heartstrings as he shrugged. "It's okay. I totally deserve it."

"No, you don't. It's not fair to take out my frustration on you because Josh stormed out of the apartment after every disagreement and left me alone for hours. Not only did it make me feel terrible, but I can't resolve an issue if you aren't here to do it. Please stay and talk me through this. Just give me a minute to wrap my head around this, please?"

North nodded but remained silent as I sorted through my feelings.

I tried to connect the dots between what he was saying and what it meant for me. "You're telling me you wrote my horoscope this morning about how I would find out upsetting news today, but it wouldn't be as bad as I might first think? That I should try to keep an open mind about how love can be expressed in unexpected ways?"

"I requested a last-minute change to run it. Originally, it was going to be about dinner with your dad. Same with mine."

Once I found out North was an Aries, I had started reading his horoscopes, too. "That's why yours said today was the day to be honest, because your selfishness hurts those you love, isn't it?"

North's expression was despondent as he stared at his clasped hands, unable to meet my gaze. "Those horoscopes were so important to you and your mom, so I didn't want to shatter your illusion about them. But I couldn't keep hiding the truth from you, either. Finding out about this years from now would ruin all your memories of us, not to mention how much worse it would hurt losing you then." He hung his head in shame. "I really believed I was being supportive by letting you continue to think some hippy-dippy lady surrounded by healing crystals and Himalayan rock salt lamps wrote them. I'm so sorry, Elias. The last thing I wanted to do was be a lying asshole like your exes, but I fucked up big-time."

Regret rolled off him in waves. It took an effort not to comfort him. I thought about his untenable position of being trapped between letting me keep believing or lying to me. He knew what honesty meant to me. Telling me the truth and changing the meaning of the last three years of Mom reading them wasn't an easy thing to confess. From his perspective, it was a lose-lose situation. If our situations were reversed, I honestly didn't know how I would handle it. Lying by sending me coded messages of encouragement to make me happy versus ruining my memories was a hell of a choice.

The longer I remained silent, the smaller he seemed to shrink on the couch. Taking a calming breath, I finally was at a place to talk through things. "I could easily get angry at you for lying to me about this and trying to manipulate me through writing the horoscopes."

"You have every right to. I'll understand if you want to break up with me and never see me again," he said, his voice cracking in his grief. The thought of losing me looked as if it physically pained him. It was comforting knowing I wasn't the only one who felt that way. "It's what I deserve for being the worst kind of asshole."

"No, trust me. I have dated the absolute worst kind of asshole. You're not Josh. He lied to me from the very beginning of our relationship, manipulated me into doing things I didn't want to do, and took advantage of my grief."

North's expression crumpled with devastation. "What are you talking about? I did the same thing. I didn't mean to, but that doesn't change the fact that I lied and tried to influence you through something you genuinely believed in."

"That's why I said I *could* get angry at you about all that. However, there are some key differences." I listed my points on my fingers. "You've never once lied to me about who you are, nor were you cheating on me with two other guys. I've known since the beginning exactly who you *are*. You just didn't know how to tell me about what you *do*."

His guilt refused to be absolved so easily. "But it's still lying by omission."

I continued outlining my thought process. "You weren't trying to manipulate me with horoscopes to force me to do things I was uncomfortable with, or didn't want to do, or punish me. All of them encouraged me to be a braver version of myself and not lock myself away in my grief. You weren't taking advantage of my pain. You were comforting me in an indirect and rather innocuous way."

"It was cute seeing how excited you got about them being accurate and coming true. All I wanted to do was make you happy."

"Do you know what my mom would have said about this?"

"That I'm an asshole charlatan who made a mockery out of something important to her and deceived her son? I should stay out of your life forever? There isn't a Hell awful enough for the likes of me?"

I guided him to look at me. His agony was far more painful than the results of his good intentions gone awry. "No, Mom would have told me that the stars foretold this and put you in my path. She would have thought the whole reason she read horoscopes was because that was how she would do her part to bring you into my life. Not only would she find this a hilarious coincidence, but she would have peppered you with a million questions about your work over dinner. She would have tried to convince you that you had more cosmic powers than you realized if you told her you were making stuff up. But most importantly, she would have insisted I didn't need to forgive you, because you did nothing wrong."

"Really?" North asked in a small voice, visibly torn up from his tumultuous emotions. "Fuck, I wish I could have met her."

"I do, too." That sad sentiment had been a dull ache in my soul the entire dinner surrounded by my mom's things at my parents' house. "I can promise that wherever she is, she's laughing about all this. She would have said—wait, I'll be right back."

Getting up and leaving behind a very confused North, I went to my bedroom to pull out the "When you meet someone special" card Mom had written me. Instead of telling him what I thought she would say, I wanted her to tell him herself. Returning to the living room, I held it out to him. "Here."

He accepted it with a puzzled look. "What's this?"

"I told you about the tradition Mom and I had of writing each other thank-you cards. Before she passed away, she also left me a box of cards for bad days, good days, and special occasions. This is the 'When you meet someone special' card I opened after you dropped me off last Sunday. I never opened it for Josh, because he didn't deserve her words. You do."

"Even though I lied to you?"

North's terror he might lose me hadn't abated. Because he seemed so wise beyond his years, it was the first time since meeting him I was struck by how young he was at twenty-two. "If I intended to break up with you over this, I wouldn't be showing you this card." I sat down next to him on the couch and gave him a gentle kiss to reassure him before looking him in the eyes to convey my sincerity. "I'm not mad at you, North, nor am I hurt. Thank you for telling me. I appreciate that you wanted to make me happy in a way that only you had the power to. I—"

Before I finished my sentence, he set aside Mom's card to pull me into a crushing hug. It surprised me he was trembling with fear. I hugged him tightly, marveling at our role reversal of me offering comfort instead of needing it from him. Weirdly, it reassured me that our relationship was balanced and not so one-sided with him always in the position of caregiver.

"Thank you, Elias. I don't know what I'd do if I lost you because of my stupidity."

I kissed his temple before nuzzling against him. "We're still good, promise."

We lingered in our embrace a few more moments before he pulled back and took out the card, smiling at the lovebirds illustration. "This might be my favorite sketch of your mom's yet."

When he opened it, the smaller pink envelope addressed "To the lucky man who loves my son" fell out onto his lap. He held it up to me, showing the holographic heart sticker seal on the back. "You haven't opened this?"

"No, but I can't wait to find out what it says. Read mine first, though."

His eyebrows shot up at the paragraph about his mother. "Oh, we *have* to tell Mom about this. She's going to lose her shit when she hears what Genevieve wrote about her."

"I'm quite certain of it."

He resumed reading, shaking his head as he continued. "Wow, she knew you best, didn't she?"

"She did," I said with a small smile. The hurt lessened knowing that I now had people like North and Callum who truly got me.

His jaw dropped as he repeated Mom's words in stunned disbelief. "'I can promise you that Mr. Right will *love* Arrietty Quenby if I have anything to do with it'? I'd be weirded out if I wasn't so damn impressed at how prescient she is. Wow, way to go, Genevieve. Seriously, we *have* to show Mom!"

"I'm okay if you want to this weekend."

"She's going to be so amazed when she sees this." He turned his attention back to finishing the rest of the card. "I know she's talking about bird North watching over you, loving you, and protecting you, but I'm going to do my part, too."

His words filled me with all kinds of warm fuzzies. "Thanks."

North picked up the envelope addressed to him. "Are you sure you want me to open this now?"

"Definitely." I circled my arm around his and leaned my head on his shoulder as I watched him take out the smaller card meant for him. We both laughed at the rough watercolor sketch of a Gouldian finch and a blue Redstart bird. "I told you she loved to draw those."

"Now Genevieve's fucking with us," North said, amusement coloring his tone. "Damn, and I thought *I* was a shameless show-off. I swear to god, if my name's in here, we're breaking out a Ouija board and having a chat with her, because this shit is batshit bonkers."

When he opened the card, I was the tiniest bit disappointed that it was addressed to "My future son-in-law" and not North.

He read it out loud. "'First and foremost, thank you for loving my wonderful son and giving him a reason to smile and laugh again. It brings me great comfort to know that he has you when I can't physically be there for him. I'm still there in spirit, but as I told Elias, I'll respectfully give you privacy during your alone time. You have my word that I'll only use my haunting powers for good, not peeping. Although, if you ever screw up and wonder why you suddenly can't find things you need, consider it well-meaning ghostly incentive to patch things up with my son.'" North chuckled at that. "Feel free to haunt the shit out of me if I fuck up, Genevieve. I'm all for an astral kick in the ass."

"Be careful what you wish for. If anyone could pull that off, it'd be her."

"I don't doubt that," he said. "'I know I don't have to tell you to be good to Elias and treat him right. If you love him, there's nothing you won't do for him. Be his sunshine who helps him thrive and grow. Help chase away those dark shadows I regrettably left him with my passing. Don't forget to also be his starlight that guides him through the darkest of nights. If you're truly the Mr. Right I helped send his way, you'll be all the things he needs simply by being you. I wouldn't let just anyone be with my son, so remember that you are already Mom-approved if you ever question your place at his side. That's no small feat for someone as picky as me. If you don't believe me, ask Elijah and Elias about my silverware or how many interior decorators I went through trying to perfect our house.'"

The comment drew a laugh from me. "She's not

kidding about that. She was *very* particular about how things should be. Dad already told you about the silverware, but the interior decorators fiasco was a whole thing."

"In your mom's defense, what she picked is incredible. As someone who has done extensive metalwork with sculptures, I appreciated the artistry."

"It was supposed to be their nice flatware they only used for company, but Dad couldn't bear the thought of going through that hassle all over again. It became our all-purpose flatware instead. Mom never found anything she liked more, but she checked stores that sold them whenever we went, just in case."

"I love that there's a story behind it. It makes them more special."

It was probably weird to be so sentimental about my family's silverware, but it was a comfort that he understood. "You're right about that."

North continued reading. "'Thank you for giving Elias a family who loves him as much as you. I'd be grateful if you found it in your hearts to include Elijah in your lives, too. He's a wonderful man who works too hard, so it might take some prying, but it would mean a lot. Since I'm sure you probably enjoy a challenge, I trust you'll find a creative way to do it.'" He grinned at that. "I definitely do. What do you think about your dad coming to our family dinners sometime? He might have fun, especially once my dad gets back from his expedition. They can go be mellow together by the fire pit outside while the rest of us get up to antics inside."

My heart swelled that North wanted my dad to be a part of their lives. "He'd like that a lot."

"Excellent. Now, let's see what other wishes of Genevieve's we can grant. 'If you happen to be an artist, please use my workshop. I have all kinds of neat stuff for you to play with that'll languish otherwise. In the unlikely event that you aren't, give tinkering a shot anyway. You might find you have an unknown talent.' Would you be okay with that?"

"If anyone deserves to use my mom's workspace, it's you. Knowing you were using her things would make me happy. I'll check with Dad, but I don't think he'll have a problem with it."

"As long as you're both fine with it, that's a gift I'll happily accept. Thanks, Genevieve. I promise I'll make something special for you. And I'll give Murray a talking to while I'm at it." I could almost hear my mom's delighted reaction to his promise to chastise her hot glue gun. "'I'm running out of room (the downside of this smaller surprise card), so I regrettably must cut this short. I still have several cards for you, so this won't be the last you'll hear from me. Have fun hunting for them in your scavenger hunt in my workshop! I'll end this by thanking you again for being the perfect Mr. Right for my son. Tragically, we won't be able to meet in person (because cancer's a real bastard), but please know I already love you.

Enjoy every precious day together that you're blessed to live a life of love with your soul mate. With much fondness and an eternal heart full of love for you, your ooky spooky future mother-in-law, Genevieve.'"

Mom's words filled me with warm fondness, almost like a hug from afar. It meant so much to me she had written that for North. I also was deeply grateful that I hadn't wasted it on Josh, who would have thrown it away and made fun of it. Not to mention how inaccurate it would have been because he had been Mr. Wrong in every single way.

Overflowing with gratitude that North had been chosen for me, I moved to straddle myself over his lap. He looked up at me with so much love that I felt like I might burst from joy. I kissed him with need, seeking entrance into his mouth as he held me tight. Everything about him was amazing, and I wanted to show him I appreciated him. I said in between kisses, "I want you so much."

"Then take me. I'm yours."

It took effort to make myself slide off him and lead him into my bedroom. He looked extra handsome in the impeccably tailored suit and corset vest that West had made for him. The curved lines of black on the blue fabric flattered his body, drawing attention to his broader shoulders, narrow waist, and pert ass. "You look so sexy in this; I almost don't want to take it off." My need to strip him naked won out over aesthetics, so I pushed off his jacket, letting it fall to the floor as we kissed. His vest didn't have buttons like a normal one, so I had to stop what I was doing to focus. "I have no idea how to remove this."

North chuckled as he turned around, presenting me with a delectable view. I ran my hands down the curve of his back, which was emphasized by the corset cinching. It was so unexpectedly sexy. I watched in fascination as he untucked strings from under the vest and loosened the cinching.

Turning to face me once more, he undid each of the hooks on the busk. He then shrugged out of it to hold out for my inspection.

I marveled at the craftsmanship of it, wondering how something so stiff could be comfortable to wear. "This really doesn't hurt?"

"Not at all. You can try it on. Our builds are similar, so it should fit."

"I'll take you up on that later." Drawing inspiration from a scene in his book, I took hold of his black tie and used it to tug him closer to me. He dropped the corset vest to the floor with an excited look. "I'm a little too preoccupied by how much I want you to do it right now." Using my grip on the thin fabric, I pulled him into a hot kiss as we ravaged each other's mouths.

My hard-on twitched in my slacks as he sensuously undid his tie, then put on a show of undoing each of his shirt buttons. After shedding my suit jacket, I mirrored his actions, too turned on to be self-conscious about putting on a striptease, especially given the fire in his eyes.

I hated having to remove my glasses but having them constantly fogging up was too annoying. It excited me to sit on top of him while he stretched out under me on the bed. It was a position neither of my exes had ever allowed me to experience, so it meant more than North realized that he let me take the lead.

Foreplay was still a novel concept to me since Will and Josh had never bothered with it. I loved getting to map out his body with my lips and fingertips, stealing tantalizing tastes of him with my tongue as I teased his nipples into hardened peaks. He rubbed my arm in silent encouragement to reassure me when I couldn't make out his face because of my crappy vision.

As I worked my way down, it presented me with a frustrating dilemma. I paused as I puzzled through it, which was exceedingly difficult given how turned on I was.

"What's wrong?"

I needed to see his expressions for that kind of conversation, so I moved up closer to his face. "I'm torn."

"About what?"

It was embarrassing to say out loud, but I did my best. "Because I should give you a blow job, but I really want to try—um, try to ride you. I've never done that, so…"

"Two things. One, hearing you say that is sexy as fuck," he told me, his voice doing an interesting growly rumble that made me almost painfully hard. "Two, there's no you 'should' about anything we ever do in bed. You don't have to blow me every time we're together."

The words were out of my mouth before I could stop them. "I don't?"

I appreciated that he didn't laugh at me. "No, you don't. Likewise, there's going to be times where we only do a blow job or a quick hand job without penetrative sex. There's not a checklist where you have to tick off each act before proceeding to the next." He rolled us over to pin me on the bed instead, but he was conscientious of remaining in my line of sight. "I will prep you, though. That's the only nonnegotiable part, because I refuse to hurt you by shoving into you like an animal. Once you're ready, we'll switch positions again so you can ride me to your heart's content, okay? There's no rule that says once you're on your back, that's where you're going to stay."

His words sent relief flooding through me. "Thank you."

"Can I ask a personal question that might be uncomfortable?"

"Uh, sure?"

He hesitated before asking in a gentle tone, "Did they hurt you when they would take you from behind when you were on your hands and knees?"

My ass clenched at the unpleasant reminder. "Always. I *hated* that position. Why?"

"Would you be comfortable letting me show you a reason to enjoy it as I prep you?" He caressed my cheek with a sympathetic look. "I promise my dick won't be anywhere near your ass. If that idea brings up too many terrible memories, forget I asked. If you want to try it and you hate what I do, I'll stop immediately and never ask again. But if you're okay with it, I'd love to give you a new pleasure and an enjoyable memory to replace the bad."

I bit my lower lip as I debated if that was a bridge I was willing to cross. "Will you use lube?"

A dark look of anger at what my question meant about my past flashed through his expressive blue eyes. "Liberally. It'll feel better than what I did with you before."

Because he had been so patient stretching me open last time, I had finally enjoyed painless sex. I could handle that, and if I couldn't, I trusted him to stop and reassure me until I felt better. "Okay."

"Are you sure?"

"I trust you. Plus, you've intrigued me."

North gave me a tender kiss that soothed my old fears. "All you have to say is 'stop' or 'no' and I swear I will."

"I know. That's why I can try."

With another kiss, he moved to grab the lube from my nightstand.

With a flutter of nervousness, I rolled over onto my hands and knees. The worst thing about that position was I couldn't see anything at all, which meant I never knew what was coming next. When I had untrustworthy partners, that had been terrifying.

Before I could ask what North was doing, he tucked a pillow under me to make me more comfortable. He didn't go straight for my hole but caressed my back to help relax me as he talked to me to keep me in the moment. "God, every part of you is fucking gorgeous. You drive me wild without trying." I tensed as he moved lower, but he kept his touch light, comforting, and above my waist. "I can't get enough of you. Do you have any idea how often I've thought about you while jerking off since leaving your place Tuesday morning after the incredible night we had?"

"A lot?"

"That's a massive understatement." He chuckled as he continued soothing me with his touch. "Thank god for lube, or my dick would be raw from overuse."

I had to laugh at that. It gave me the confidence to admit, "I've never been more grateful for the private bathrooms at the office."

"You did it at work?"

The interest in his voice made it easier to talk about. "I'm used to feeling awful for days afterward. Having a pleasant ache the next day was a new experience for me. It kept reminding me of what we did, which was unexpectedly arousing."

"Fuck, that's so goddamn sexy," he groaned, as he glided over my ass for a gentle grope. "Thanks for giving me something new to fantasize about. You in a suit jerking off at work while thinking of us? *Fuck*."

North ran his hands down my thighs, before easing up the inside of them. I inhaled when he cupped my balls and teased them. It felt so good I thrust against the pillow for some relief. I mourned when he moved his hand away, trailing it upward to gently spread my cheeks. My breathing hitched as he brushed against my entrance.

While I trusted him, my body tensed up from the awful memories associated with my current position. He broke the tension when he put his lips against one of my cheeks.

I asked through laughter, "Did you kiss my ass?"

He pressed his smirk against my skin so I could feel it. "I sure did." He placed another peck on the opposite cheek. "Yours is the only ass I'm happy to kiss any day of the week."

I snorted in amusement. "Seriously?"

"Absolutely." He kissed my hole, which drew an interesting sound out of me. "There isn't one place on you I wouldn't gratefully worship for the rest of my life."

"Why would you kiss me there, though?"

"Because it's beautiful." North ran his tongue over my pucker, causing me to squeak from the unexpected sensation. "Because I love every single inch of you."

My words wouldn't come out right. "D-did you —*there*?"

"Mm-hmm." North swirled his tongue in a circle around my most intimate of areas, before placing another kiss on it with the tiniest hint of suction. It did funny things to my heart and stomach. "I told you, I want to give you a new pleasure."

My next attempt at a sentence disappeared when he lapped at it, then flicked it with his tongue. I was unprepared for him to spread me a little wider and dip into me. The strange sensation made me yelp in shock. "W-what kind of pleasure is that?"

"A rim job, to be technical about it." I could hear him grinning. "Eating your ass if I want to be crude."

I turned to look at him over my shoulder out of habit, despite him being an indistinct blur. "Why would you do that?"

"Because it feels fucking amazing."

"But isn't that gross?"

"Not to me." North resumed caressing my sides to comfort me. "If you don't want me to do that, I won't."

It took a moment to gather my composure to answer. "I'm not sure if I like it or not. It's…" I couldn't settle on an appropriate description. "Different?"

"Do you want another demonstration to help you figure it out, or should I stop?"

"You really enjoy it?" That was the hardest part to wrap my mind around.

"Hell yeah."

It felt strange to request him to continue, but now that I knew what he was doing, maybe I might enjoy it. "You can keep going."

North kissed my ass cheek before spreading me open. He took his time licking to get me used to the sensation before he delved in again. I clutched the sheets in my hands as he started tonguing me earnestly, moaning as he did so. It was beyond me how he derived any pleasure from that, but I could hear it in his sounds of satisfaction.

I dropped my head as I surrendered to the sensations. With my eyes closed, it sharpened my focus on what he was doing. The teasing thrusts of his tongue combined with the way he would lightly suck on my hole before dipping in felt incredible. In fact, it was so enjoyable, I didn't want him to stop until I came. Before I passed the point of no return, I made myself say, "Stop."

He immediately did, his hands once more touching me gently above the waist to reassure me. "Okay."

I could hear the concern in his tone, so I reassured him. "I'm fine. I stopped you because it feels *too* good, not because it's bad."

That drew a laugh out of him. "Is there such a thing?"

"I'm not ready for it to be over."

"Even if you come, it's nowhere close to being over."

He had more than proven that to me, but it was important to me to come while I rode him. "Next time, great. But this time, I want to wait."

"As you wish. Do you need a break before I use lube to ready you?"

Taking a few calming breaths to recenter myself, I consented. "I can handle that."

North slid lubed fingers into me, stretching me open while being careful to avoid hitting the most sensitive spot. After he fit three of them comfortably, he asked, "Are you okay to move on?"

"Yeah."

He withdrew and helped me roll over to reposition on top of him. After he put on a condom, he encouraged me, "Take it slow and remember to breathe. We're not in any rush."

Nodding, I eased onto his rigid length, grateful when he guided it into me. As I lowered myself, he stroked my thighs to help keep me grounded and soothe me as I took it at my own pace. It took an ungodly amount of time before I bottomed out. I remained motionless as I adjusted, exhaling in relief that I was fine. There was no blinding pain, only a sense of fullness and connection with North.

Mentally, I still expected to get snapped at to speed things up and quit wasting time, but he never did. He reached up and caressed my sides as he asked in a gentle voice, "Doing okay?"

"Mm-hmm." I tensed my muscles around him, causing him to tighten his grip on my hips. The possessiveness of the gesture sent a thrill through me. "Can I move now?"

"If you're comfortable."

In his hands, I didn't just feel comfortable, I felt *safe*. Tentatively shifting, I started off with small movements as I got used to the position. It wasn't immediately pleasurable, but it didn't hurt, which was a definite plus. As I grew more confident, I moved more deliberately.

My first glimpse of what was in store for me came when North pushed up to meet me on a downward bounce. It had me scrambling for a hold on something. He guided my hands to rest on his stomach, helping me balance as I picked up the pace. The next time he thrust into me, I gasped as it sent lust ricocheting through my system. It got better when he grabbed my ass and used his grip to help guide my hips as we found our rhythm.

In chasing after the sensations, I left my fears and doubts in the dust. I tossed my head back and closed my eyes as I focused on *feeling*. I was awash in the bombardment of sensual stimulation as everything blurred into white-hot heat. Moans escaped from me, spurred on by every sigh and swear that fell from North's lips. My enjoyment was further heightened as his hands wandered, tweaking my nipples before caressing me all over. I gave myself over to the experience, losing myself in how incredible the moment was.

It came as a complete shock to my system when North started working my hardness. I shouted as it sent me flying higher, the dual pleasures almost more than I could handle.

Overwhelmed, I raced toward the cliff of my climax, but I wasn't there yet. Shifting forward hoping to find the right spot made me growl in frustration when the angle didn't do it for me. I squinted as I tried to make out North's face to judge how the experience was for him, despite it being impossible.

He sat up, causing me to cry out when it helped him hit something that made my toes curl. I buried my fingers in his hair as I held on to him for dear life, my body ceaselessly moving as the promising tingling built up inside me. Every touch sent me spiraling into a dizzying, lustful spiral as I got closer to my edge.

"So good," I whimpered, my enjoyment further enhanced by being able to visually confirm he was in heaven like me. Not to mention the consideration that he had noticed I had been trying to see him and sat up to be close enough that I could. "Oh, North!"

It caught me off guard when my calling out his name made him come with a gasp. I stopped moving, making everything inside me scream when I was *so close*.

"Why'd you stop?"

"Because you came." That had always meant game over with my exes, who ceased to care whether I got off after that point.

"I don't stop until you come, too." He resumed jerking me off as he sensually kissed along my neck. "Keep going."

The fact that he wanted me to continue after he got off was unbelievable. I lost it when he tugged on my ear with his teeth as he brushed his thumb over the head of my cock. I climaxed hard, marking his stomach with my release.

I rested my forehead against his, trying to recover my breath and equilibrium from the intense euphoria. He hugged me closer, making me melt into a satisfied puddle as he murmured how much he loved me. I nuzzled against him as I indulged in the afterglow and his gentle touch that kept sending little jolts of pleasure zinging through me. I couldn't believe he let me finish after he came first.

Part of me really wanted to kiss him, but I also needed him to brush his teeth first after his thorough rim job. I settled for kissing his neck with a satisfied sigh as I rested my head on his shoulder. We remained in a silent embrace, even after he slipped out of me. In his arms, his love obliterated all the terrible things that had come before with Will and Josh.

Aware that I was lingering past the point of

acceptability, I quietly asked, "How long can I stay like this?"

"Until you tell me to go brush my teeth so I can kiss you like I'm dying to, then use cleaning as an excuse to keep touching you before I snuggle you to sleep."

I laughed, light and free from my powerful release. "You make a very convincing argument for me to move."

North hugged me tighter. "Stay a little longer."

"How about forever?"

"Forever isn't long enough, but it's a good start."

I smiled as I basked in being with someone you loved with all your heart and then some. It was impossible to be certain whether Mom, the stars, or the cosmic universe really had a hand in bringing North into my life. The only thing I knew without a shadow of a doubt was that I was the luckiest man alive to be loved by him.

Epilogue

NORTH

TWO WEEKS LATER

ANNIVERSARIES HAD ALWAYS SEEMED cheesy as hell to me, but every day I was lucky enough to be with Elias was worth celebrating. Maybe it was silly to do something special for it, but I couldn't resist. After a wonderful dinner, I pulled out a rainbow-colored holographic box from my bag and gave it to him.

"What's this?"

"Something special to celebrate our one-month anniversary."

He blushed at my words. "You didn't have to get me anything."

"I didn't get you something. I made you something."

It was cute seeing him brighten with excitement.

"Thank you, but I don't have anything for you. I didn't know we were doing gifts."

"Getting to see your reaction is your anniversary gift to me."

Elias untied the iridescent metallic ribbon bow and took off the lid, then unfolded the glitter tissue paper to reveal what was inside. He gasped as he pulled out my present. I had made a bird out of his mother's special silverware. The curved parts of the spoons formed the head, back, and chest. I used the fork prongs for the wings, and the butter knife for the tail. The distinctive two-toned silver-and-gold handles were perfect for the eyes, especially once I glued on blue irises I had found in Genevieve's workshop where I had made him.

I considered it my ultimate masterpiece, but I got nervous about Elias's silence as he stared at it in shock. "Since we're together, I thought clockwork North deserved a boyfriend of his own."

My heart did an entire gymnastics routine when he reached out and pet the bird's head with the cutest smile I had ever seen. "He's so beautiful," he said in an awed voice. I breathed a sigh of relief that he wasn't upset that I had repurposed his mom's flatware. "How did you make this?"

"When we went to your dad's house for dinner, I asked if I could have some of your mom's silverware to make your gift. He happily gave them to me with his and Genevieve's blessing. I practiced on some shitty stuff first, because there was no way I was risking messing your mom's up."

He stroked him again. "What's his name?"

"What do you think about East? It starts with the same letter as yours, plus they're closer than North and South. I thought about maybe Vieve after your mom, but I'm still hoping you'll use that for drag someday."

Elias laughed as he gestured for me to follow him into the bedroom where he kept the sculpture his mom had made as her last birthday gift to him. He set the silverware bird next to him on the dresser and made introductions. "North, this is East. Now you'll have someone, too." He smiled up at me. "I hope they'll be as happy as us."

"I'm certain they will be. They were made for each other, just like us." I pulled Elias into a hug, then gave him a tender kiss. "Happy one-month anniversary."

"The first of many happy anniversaries." He looked at me with so much love that my heart overflowed with a joy I hadn't known was possible. "I love you, North."

"I love you, too." Grinning, I couldn't resist teasing him. "Do I need to turn them around the other way so they don't see us celebrating our anniversary? Or are we going to teach them a thing or two about the birds and the bees?"

It was impossible to hold in my laugh when Elias

moved both birds to avert their eyes from what we were about to do. Every little thing about him made me fall more and more in love with him, especially his cute quirks. I was grateful for everything that had brought us together, whether it be fate or coincidence. Every day was a gift that I treasured, and I couldn't wait to spend the rest of our lives with each other.

How do Elias and North celebrate their first anniversary? **Claim your copy of Infinity of Stars to find out today**.

Want to see Felix's romantic vacation of a lifetime in Paris? **Read Picture Love next to enjoy his swoony romance with the dashing Arsène**.

Want to see where the Sunnyside universe begins? **Check out Bet on Love to start the adventure**.

Thank You

Thank you for reading **Love Directions**. Reviews are crucial for helping other readers discover new books to enjoy. If you want to share your love for Elias and North, please leave a review. I'd really appreciate it!

Recommending my work to others is also a huge help. Don't hesitate to give this book a shout-out in your favorite book rec group to spread the word.

Next in Series

AVAILABLE NOW

A Paris vacation with his friend's sexy older brother playing tour guide is Felix's idea of the perfect getaway. Will Arsène be a fun fling or the greatest love of Felix's life?

Felix Murphy

I'm living the dream when my friend's hot, older brother with a swoony French accent plays tour guide for me in Paris. I certainly won't complain if Arsène adds his bedroom to the itinerary of places we should visit. If I'm really lucky, maybe he'll teach me lessons in the fine art of French kissing while we're seeing the sights together.

As long as I don't go home with a broken heart for a souvenir, what's the harm in having some fun with a sexy vacation fling?

Arsène Devereaux

I expected showing my younger brother's American friend around my hometown to be a painful way to spend my day off. But Felix is a playful flirt who makes me want to show him why Paris is called the City of Love. To my surprise, I need more than just a week alone with him.

What if our fun could continue even after he returns home?

Picture Love is the sixth book in the ***Good Bad Idea*** series and part of the Sunnyside universe. This novel features a brother's best friend, insta love, age gap, gay romance. If you love cute sweetness, sexy fun, and low angst stories that will make you laugh and swoon, you'll adore this satisfying **HEA** without cliffhangers. Each book can be read as a standalone or as part of the series in order.

Also by Ariella Zoelle

For a complete and up-to-date list of Ariella Zoelle's low angst releases, please visit her website at

www.ariellazoelle.com/ariella-zoelle-all

Also by A.F. Zoelle

In the mood for something with more angst and drama?
Check out A.F. Zoelle's dark romances at

www.ariellazoelle.com/af-zoelle-all

Acknowledgments

This has been one hell of a year in so many different ways, hasn't it? This **Good Bad Idea** series has by far been the best part of it for me, because I've been able to connect with so many enthusiastic readers and share in the joy. It's really helped keep me going through these tough times while I try to balance work and my publishing life after leaving academia. I'm so thankful to everyone who has taken the time to reach out and let me know how much they've adored this series.

I want to give a special shout-out to Amy Mitchell whose warmth, kindness, and enthusiasm have truly touched me. She's not only become a good friend, but she's an amazing beta reader. I'm also thankful for Beth Barton, whose keen eyes caught a minor oops in my previous book. I'm grateful for the opportunity to get to know them and the other members of my Facebook group.

I'm so appreciative for my dream team of Pam, Sandra, and Cate both of whom are absolute gems and come through for me every time.

I also want to thank Katie from Gay Romance

Reviews and all of the ARC readers who have been so generous with their encouraging words! It's made a world of difference for helping get my name out there. I feel so lucky that every release manages to be more successful than the last, and it's due in large part to their efforts.

I can't wait to meet again in **Picture Love**!

About the Author

ariella zoelle
WWW.ARIELLAZOELLE.COM

Ariella Zoelle adores steamy, funny, swoony romances where couples are allowed to just be happy. She writes low angst stories full of heat, humor, and heart. But sometimes she's in the mood for something with a bit more angst and drama. If you are too, check out her A.F. Zoelle books.

Get a bonus chapter by using the QR code below!

Printed in Great Britain
by Amazon